Sisters

A novel

by

Tom Creary

ISBN: 978-0-9921520-4-8

To my Dad, resting in peace all these years

Other novels by Tom Creary

The Bohemian Connection (2013)

The Lady from Toledo (2014)

The Russian Intrusion (2016)

Survivor (2017)

Chapter 1

Ronsperg, Bohemia, Austro-Hungarian Empire, 1860

The cavalry officer walked through the gate of the castle and down the hill to the string of cottages. He thought he remembered which one was his cousin's. It would be the cleanest and tidiest of the twenty or so that dotted the plateau above the valley. He observed the rolling hills and the rows of poplar trees and hedges that formed the boundaries of the fields of the great estate. He strode down the center lane, saw the little white house with the crafted heavy oak door, and the freshly painted red window frames. Josef's. Yes. It will be his.

He knocked on the door and it quickly opened. His cousin was there, beaming with a big smile on his face. "Franz, what a surprise. Come in. Come in. Please. And to what do we owe this honor?"

Franz Schropfer, captain in the elite cavalry of the Imperial Army of Austria-Hungary, walked in and hugged the man he had not seen in nearly four years. "I'm here to visit. It's been a long time. Not since your wedding. I wanted to know how you were. My unit is camped at the castle. We were on training maneuvers near Hostau. I hope I am not imposing."

"No, of course not. Rosaline, please come. Franz is here. You must stay for dinner, by the way" Josef said, as he turned back toward his cousin. "Is that possible? You can't arrive like this without having dinner with us." Rosaline emerged with their little boy, George, in her arms.

"Franz, such a long time since we have seen you," she said. "Here, you see the little one. Meet George." The shy child turned and put his head on his mother's shoulder.

"Very handsome boy. Congratulations. I suppose there are more coming?" said Franz with a twinkle in his eye.

"Yes, of course. If my husband continues to want me," replied the pretty young woman with a wry smile on her face.

"Now, now, my dear" said Josef. "We must be discreet about these things. Can we talk about dinner? Franz will be joining us."

"Yes, I have a big chicken in the back, a hen that doesn't produce so many eggs anymore. We will have her with some other good things. Take George while I prepare it all. Again, Franz, so glad to see you. Josef has such great respect for you. You must know that. Welcome back." Before Franz could respond, she put the little boy down and retreated to the kitchen.

Later, after dinner and discussions about the family and life in the cavalry of the Emperor, his postings to seemingly every corner of the vast domain, and after Rosaline had left the table to put the child to bed, Franz looked at his cousin. "Josef, what are you doing now? You were part of the farm here before. Now you are not. It is obvious. Your hands are not callused or rough as they used to be. What does the estate have you do now? The cottage here is part of the estate. You don't own it, do you?"

"No, I don't own the cottage, Franz. Of course not. That is for sure. The estate owns them all. I have very little in terms of possessions, actually, but at least I don't do the back-breaking work anymore. I handle the accounts of the estate. I am the bookkeeper, if you wish."

"How did you do that? Go from farm worker to bookkeeper of the estate? As I remember, you only had a couple years of school. What happened? That's quite something."

"Yes. Bookkeeper. I decided a few years ago I did not want to be an ignorant farm peasant all my life, so I decided to learn how to read properly. I did that. And then learned some things about business. There is a retired professor here in the village. He decided to help me. When he saw that I could read, he gave me some books on how to do accounting as well as other aspects of managing a business. I read them. Then, three years or so ago, I learned that the head of the estate was unhappy with the bookkeeper he had. I went to see him. I said I could do the job if he would give me a chance. He was surprised. He had always seen me as one of his peasants working the land. But, he said he had a problem. He needed somebody quickly and that I had a week to show him I could do the job. That's how it happened."

"He is a good boss to you, Josef? The Schiffen family has a reputation for meanness. Just like so many aristocratic families. I had an unpleasant discussion with him this afternoon, actually, about our unit using his stable for the night. He was not nice. I told him the accommodation should be considered a service to the Emperor. He backed off."

"I am not surprised. He is not nice. Regularly dresses people down. It can be humiliating. I endure it. The alternative is returning to hard work in the fields and a much lower wage."

Franz, the gallant officer who was like a brother to Josef when they were young, was quick to respond. "Josef, you have to get out of here. To Vienna, or somewhere else, better than here.

The world is changing. There are opportunities for people with ambition."

"How can I do that? I don't know anyone in Vienna. The people I know are all around here. I'm thirty years old now. I'm stuck here, my good cousin," responded Josef.

"I know people. I can help you. We were always close when we were boys. I was lucky to be the son of a military officer, a privileged person as a graduate of the Imperial War College. Our side of the family has had it much easier. I have often felt bad about that, knowing that you and my other cousins did not have the same opportunity as I had. Let me help you. You are too good a man to languish in this little place, with these damn aristocrats who keep people in submission and poverty."

"You are a good man, Franz. Your men must appreciate you."

"I am not always so sure of that. Being a responsible officer and leader of men is not so easy. Taking orders from generals who get their positions more from influence than capability can also be difficult. But I am lucky, and I have a wonderful wife, just like you."

"How is Lizzy, by the way?" asked Josef.

"She is wonderful. I am blessed."

"But no children yet, Franz. Unless you have one you haven't told us about."

"No. No children. We will not have any. Lizbeth cannot have children. Maybe we can help our cousins' children."

"I'm sorry to hear that."

"It is God's will. But, let me work on getting you and Rosa to Vienna. Now, I must leave. I have to check my men and see if there are any problems with Herr Schiffen before the end of the evening. I will be in touch with you soon. Good night, and say goodbye to Rosa for me."

A month later, Josef received a letter from Franz. 'Dear Josef, I have arranged an interview for you with one of the managing directors of the main bank here in Vienna. I have known him for some time. I told him about you, your being self-taught and ambitious enough to get out of the drudgery of farm work to become the bookkeeper for one of the largest estates in Bohemia. When I told him it was the von Schiffen estate, he said that he wanted to meet you. All about silver, I gather. He proposes a meeting Monday at his office three weeks from now. Find a way to get here. His name and the address of the office are listed below. It is in your hands now. This will good for you. I will see you when you are here. Franz.'

The train arrived from Prague. Josef emerged from the sprawling station and observed the magnificence of the buildings all around, the fine carriages, and the elegantly dressed people on the street. He found the pension that Franz had recommended and after checking in, walked around the center of the city. Turning a corner, he saw an elegantly crafted iron gate with a huge building a hundred meters further across a wide expanse of lawn. He walked further and saw that the building extended far down the street. He stopped someone and asked what the building was. The Hofburg Palace, said the man. The Palace of the Emperor. It never seemed to end. Statues with men in uniform on horses dotted the property and the perimeter of the buildings with many sections crafted in the ornate, elegant, massive architecture of the place. Josef in his awe had stepped off the walkway on the perimeter of the grounds and was nearly run over by a four-horse carriage carrying a group of plumed passengers. Important people. He looked at his clothes. They were nowhere near the quality and cut of the clothes of the men walking beside him on the street. Vienna, he thought. So far from what I know. Do I want this? He stopped, found a café and went in. Like everything else he had seen that afternoon, the café had elegance and grandeur. A small orchestra played a waltz. Waiters in starched collars, cravats, waistcoats and pressed trousers plied among the tables, serving coffee, teas and pastries. Another world, he thought.

He arrived early the next day for his meeting. The bank was on the corner of the immense square of St. Stephen's Cathedral, and across the street from what he would learn was the stock exchange building which housed many of the financial houses of the Empire. Creditanstalt was for all practical purposes the only bank of Austria. Emperor Franz Joseph had favored the bank and its monopoly of financial affairs in the Empire ever since he had ascended the throne, even though a Jewish family, the Rothschilds, and not a Catholic one, controlled it.

"You are a specialist in silver. That is what you must be if you do the bookkeeping for the von Schiffen family," said the man.

"Yes, I know something of silver. It is the basis of the wealth of the family. The agricultural side of the operations is important but as you imply, silver provides the major revenues of the estate. From mining activities in Bohemia and Moravia. It is well known. I am not divulging any secrets. I do all of the mining operations bookkeeping and negotiate many of the transactions as well."

"Your education, Herr Tauer. Tell me about it. People who work for me, apart from the clerks and messengers, must have adequate instruction, be able to read, write, be able to understand economic and political affairs, converse intelligently."

"I have but two years of formal schooling. My family was poor. I had to go to work at a young age. I taught myself how to read and write, and later learned the principles of accounting and business from a retired professor in our village who took me under his wing. I was fortunate to have that. I don't know what Captain Schropfer told you about me. I would be glad to answer any questions, sir. It would be an honor for me to work for you."

"Well, my friend the captain said you were his cousin and that he could vouch for you. We have known each for a long time and I respect his views on people as well as on many other things. He said you knew a lot about silver. That you were self-educated with good character and good habits, and that you spoke English, which is important for us here. It weighs heavily in your favor if that is the case."

"Very well. I indeed do speak English, as you say. I learned it on my own, with help from the professor I just spoke about, as the estate has dealings with buyers in England and someone had to communicate with them. I accompany Herr von Schiffen to meetings with Englishmen in Berlin and Prague. Not many Englishmen speak or read German. What would you want me to do here, sir?" asked Josef.

"Work with us in managing our holdings and exposure to silver. It is the basis of the currency of the Empire. We must manage it well. You would do the same for the bank that you have apparently been doing for the von Schiffen family. You would work for the director of the section. One of his key people became ill recently and will not return. Here are the duties you would be expected to perform…Are you interested? It would mean coming here to Vienna, of course."

"Yes, I am interested. I must ask you what the salary would be. I have a family," said Josef.

"Of course, the salary….." The man quoted the amount that the position paid to begin with and the conditions under which increases would be awarded over time. "Is this acceptable, Herr Tauer?"

"Yes. That would be acceptable." It was far more than he could ever expect to earn with the Schiffen family.

"Well, then. I am willing to hire you. Could you start towards the end of next month? Say, five weeks from now. That should give you time to organize your affairs. Could we do that?"

"Yes, I think so. I will have to find a place for the family to live here, but I think I can manage that."

The train rolled through the Bohemian countryside. Going to work for the bank of the Empire, of the Emperor, he thought. Hard to believe. So, so far from the village, from what I have known. The professor told me about luck, about recognizing opportunity. What did he say? 'Some people don't know an opportunity if it would strike them in the forehead. A peasant may never come across one to better his life. You may be lucky, Josef. When one comes to you, recognize it, seize it.' I did with Schiffen and I will do it again. Thank God for the professor. Opportunity. Don't ruin it, Josef. He thought of his boyhood and his father. His father who told him to be determined to do better than he. He would do it.

It was late, just before midnight. The trip back had taken a day and a half. Three train and two carriage rides. He was lucky to have arrived in Pilsen on time to catch the last carriage that served the villages leading to the border with Bavaria. Ronsperg was the last stop. There a light on. Every other house was dark. Rosaline still up, he thought. Josef opened the door, saw his wife sitting in the stuffed chair in the parlor room, knitting, but before she could say anything, he blurted out, "My dear, we have a new life ahead of us. We will be going to Vienna."

"Vienna. We know nothing of Vienna, Josef. Are you sure of this?" asked Rosaline as he crossed the floor and embraced her. "I have a position with the biggest bank of the empire, starting in a few weeks, my dear. An incredible chance this is, an opportunity to have a better life, infinitely better than staying here. I will never have another chance like this. Thanks to Franz. I am sure of it."

Things were racing through her mind. She had never in her short life been further than twenty kilometers from the doorstep of where she was at that moment.

"Where will we live? My parents, what will become of them? They will be upset. So far away for them."

"Rosa, for living in Vienna, Franz is helping us already. He is looking for us. And as to your parents, they can come with us, if they wish. Your father is still relatively young and robust. He could find work in Vienna. Tending horses there is not much different from tending horses here. Vienna is booming. He will certainly find something. We can propose that to them. My dear, this is a new life for us."

"You will have to tell Schiffen. What will he say? He will not want you to leave. He could make it difficult for you."

"I will see. I will see him tomorrow."

"Well, Tauer, this is unexpected." Count Rudolf von Schiffen was not happy. No one left the employ of the estate without his permission. He controlled the surrounding area and he was used to controlling the people who lived in it as well. He hired and he fired. People did not leave of their own accord. Certainly not without repercussions. But, this was perhaps different. Tauer would be working for the bank that bought his silver. "I must think about it. You and your family have worked here for generations. You handle sensitive matters. I will have to take it up."

"I am sorry, Herr Schiffen. You have been proper with me and my family over time. But I wish to move on. I hope you can accept that." I am stretching the truth, but I must do it, thought Josef. Be nice and thank him.

"Well, I will have to take this into consideration. You have much information about our affairs. There are matters of confidentiality. We will speak again at the beginning of the week. In the meantime, you have work to do. You were gone for four days. You said you were ill. You were in Vienna. You were not truthful with me. We will speak. Good day, Herr Tauer."

"He is not going to let me do this. It is not going to be easy. We may have to just leave, Rosa, and your parents will have to come with us." Josef was back home after his meeting with von Schiffen. He dreaded going to work that afternoon and the days after that.

On the following Monday, Tauer was in the castle office in front of the scion of the domain. "You can go, Tauer. I have thought about it. This could actually be something positive for the estate. I need to have good relations with the bank. You could ensure me of that. We could continue to work together. Ja? Nothing unlawful or indiscreet, but a working relationship, just the same." It was a question, not a statement, thought Josef. "If I need to know things, could I ask you? Could we do that?"

What has he been organizing? Has he communicated with the bank? Josef was relieved, but suspicious. The man had expectations. I may be leaving Ronsperg, but Herr von Schiffen wants to retain control. One step at a time. "Thank you, sir. I am sorry to be leaving your employ. I will do my best to respond to you as long as I do not violate the conditions of my employment with the bank. I will be respectful of your needs as much as I can."

"Well, I can't really prevent you from leaving. You are free to go. May we stay in good relations. In the meantime, you can leave next week, if you wish. Could you spend the rest of this week informing Klauner of your duties? He knows a lot of it, but I need you to ensure a good transition."

"Yes sir, of course. Thank you, sir. Good day."

Josef went to the telegraph office that afternoon and sent a telegram to the man at the bank saying he could start earlier if he wished, and that he would be in Vienna to try to secure a place to live the following Monday. The return telegraph the next day said that he would be free to start whenever he could move his family and that he would be available to meet with Josef whenever he arrived. He was to simply come to the office and he would make himself available.

"Herr Tauer, welcome. I wish you well with us. I must say, however, that your employer, von Schiffen, came to see my boss last week," said the man when Josef arrived at his office. "He was directed to me. He was not happy. He tried to get me to withdraw my offer to you, but I decided to maintain it and I told him. He was not nice and that bothered me. It is time we did away with indentured service. I told him we value the relationship with the von Schiffen family, but that we seek to have the best people work for us. I told him I would not withdraw the offer for you. He left in a bit of a huff."

"I thank you, sir. It has not been easy working for the man and I suspected he may have come here. Herr von Schiffen wants me to maintain a communication with him. He expects to retain control over people. It is his way. I said I would try to accommodate him, but that my loyalty would have to be with my new employer."

"You will have to be careful about that, Herr Tauer. You will be working for us now. The von Schiffen estate is a major supplier of silver to the bank and we must maintain a good relationship. Let me know if there are attempts to obtain undue favors. That being said, welcome to the bank. You may start whenever you are ready. I have secured for you a small amount to cover your travel expenses coming here and all. It is a policy of the bank, to facilitate having people from the regions work for us. Important for doing business throughout the Empire. Before you leave this afternoon, I will introduce you to the head of the section. He is anxious to meet you. You know the workings of the supply side of the silver business. It is important for him and for us. Just be careful with Herr von Schiffen."

Within three weeks, Josef and Rosaline had moved to Vienna. Franz had quickly found a place for them. The rent was acceptable and the house was large enough to accommodate Rosaline's parents. Josef's brother and two sisters and Rosaline's siblings, most of whom were older than she, stayed at Ronsperg. But they could now come to Vienna to visit and be exposed to something other than the slow pace of life in rural Bohemia and they did. The Tauer home over time became a way station for brothers, sisters and cousins who could make it to the city for visits. Josef and Rosaline spent much time with Franz and his wife Lizbeth, who doted on little George. Lizbeth had become an artist, painting portraits of people, including her husband, in their homes or in outdoor settings. One of her large paintings was of Franz as cavalry officer on his mount as he prepared for a military parade. Plumed helmet, red sash across the chest, sword in the air, the magnificent white stallion. The painting would become celebrated in Viennese art circles as a portrayal of the gallantry of the Austrian military class. Lizbeth loaned it to a public art gallery across the street from the royal palace. It was said that Rudolf, the Habsburg heir and only son of the Emperor, went a number of times to the gallery specifically to show the painting to friends and had enquired as to purchasing it. The owner told him it was not for sale. Lizbeth had been firm about that.

Josef and Rosaline gradually felt more comfortable in Viennese society. They would never be regarded as being part of the privileged class; that was impossible given their origins, but life in Vienna proved to be good and they prospered from it. They went to the cafes for tea and pastries on weekends, sometimes to the theatre, leaving George with Rosa's parents. The countryside and Ronsperg were a long way away in more ways than one.

Over the first few years in Vienna, Rosaline had two other children, the first one, a boy, who died soon after birth, and the second, a little girl who succumbed to diphtheria before her first birthday. Little George remained the only child, at least for awhile. In the meantime, Josef worked at the bank and became the top working specialist in Vienna in the business of silver. He was promoted to head of the section upon the retirement of the incumbent a few years after his arrival. Silver was the mainstay of the currencies of virtually every country of Europe, including Prussia, England, France and Russia. The mines of the Empire in Moravia, Bohemia, Slovenia and Transylvania supplied much of the needs of the governments of the continent. The same applied to the major European industrial concerns that had to deal in hard currencies for the purchase of their raw materials.

Chapter 2

July 1866…..

Tensions that had been building for years between Prussia and Austria erupted into war that summer of 1866. Battles were being fought in southern Germany, in Bohemia and in Italy, which had allied itself with Prussia.

Josef opened the door. It was 7:30 on a Sunday morning. "Lizzy, what is this? Is there something wrong? You look distressed."

"Franz. He's in Bohemia. There was a battle yesterday. At a place called Koniggratz. Reports are saying they were defeated with many casualties. I have no news about him. I fear the worst. I needed to be with someone. I came here."

"Of course. Come in."

Lizbeth would soon learn that Franz had been captured and that his unit had been virtually wiped out. Only Franz and one other man from his regiment had survived the charge that day. They were both prisoners. She would have no other news from him for weeks. One day she received a short letter, saying that he was being treated fairly, but that he had lost an arm in the battle. He gave his love and said he hoped to return home soon. In the meantime, the war had ended.

With the peace treaty signed soon after the battle of Koniggratz, Austria-Hungary was relegated to what amounted to secondary status in Europe. Prussia, with Bismarck as leader, would form a new German Confederation and become the most powerful country on the continent.

A month later....

Someone was knocking on the door. Josef opened it. It was Lizbeth. "Franz has been released, Josef. He is coming home. He will be here in a couple of days. I just received word from the War Department."

"Come in. We can talk inside," said Josef as people were passing by on the street.

"I will not stay long," she said after entering. "But I fear the worst. He lost an arm. I wonder what other injuries he may have."

"Well, he's alive. That's what's important. He is a strong man. Let us know when he arrives. We will go see you."

"Very well. I wanted you to know. It is not a long walk to come here. Thank you, Josef. You have been very kind to me."

Josef was shocked. His gallant, robust and imposing cousin had lost at least forty pounds. He was thin, gaunt, with only one arm. He limped as well, with a wound to his leg that was not healing well.

"What happened, Franz? Can you talk about it?"

"We had no chance. We were outmaneuvered, out officered and outfought. We had more guns, more cavalry and the advantage of being on our own territory. We squandered it all. You want to know why, I suppose."

"Well yes, I do. Are the Prussians so much better?" asked Josef.

"It has to do with the fundamentals of our military structure. Our army has created its own weaknesses. They all came together to lead to our defeat. A humiliating one. The leaders will not admit these weaknesses, but they are real. Four things....just to begin with, Josef. One, nine languages are spoken in our infantry, and in most of the cavalry as well. Virtually all of the officers are Austrian and speak German. Most of their men don't even understand what they are being told. Imagine what that can mean on the battlefield. Two, we bring soldiers into the army and then let them go home after training to tend to their farms or whatever. When they are brought back, in mobilization for war or whatever, they essentially need to be re-trained, re-disciplined, put back into fighting shape. So inefficient. Three, the army stations its soldiers in other regions from where they come from. A soldier from Slovenia will be stationed in Moravia. A soldier from Moravia will be stationed in Bosnia. This, of course, in this ethnic mix of an empire, is to avoid them getting induced to participate in any local independence movement or whatever of their home region. It is the ultimate fear of the Emperor - a revolt of the peoples. So, mobilization takes far more time because of it, with soldiers coming from all over to join their units with usually a long time passing since they were trained. Transportation becomes a chaotic mess. It was for this battle and for this war. Language problems magnify the problem of organization. Despite our superiority in numbers and having the high ground, many of the infantry units were under-manned. It was chaos. Four, we have rifles that are muzzle loading. One has to stand up to reload, exposing oneself to enemy fire. The

Prussians have none of the first three problems and have breech loading rifles that can be reloaded while lying down. Put those four together and that is why we lost this war and will lose others unless things change."

It was a Thursday afternoon. Josef was at his office. "Herr Tauer, there is a lady here to see you. She insists on speaking with you."

"Did she give her name?"

"Yes. Frau Lizbeth Schropfer. She said you are related."

"Show her in. Thank you, Schmidt." What could be the problem? This is not like her. Something must be happening. Something serious, he thought.

"Josef, Franz has been arrested. For cowardice and dereliction of duty. At Koniggratz. This is unbelievable. I don't know what to think."

"My Lord. Cowardice? Franz? It can't be."

"He has lost his commission as well. Not only is he under arrest, he is no longer an officer in the army. I don't know what to do. Can I come to stay with you and Rosaline? Would you mind?"

"Of course you can. But what happened? How did this come about? What has Franz told you?"

"He said to me, the other evening before he was arrested, that the army is seeking scapegoats for losing the war. He said that word was out that the Emperor and the cabinet are furious and looking for blood. People all over the empire are upset at losing the war. The Emperor needs culprits. The War Minister was sacked two weeks ago, as you know. Franz told me that evening that other heads would roll. He has become one of them, Josef."

"Scapegoats. Yes. I remember what Franz told me when he came back, about the inefficiencies of the army."

"He was a loyal officer. He led a charge. He told me about it. Infantry were supposed to follow the charge. They didn't. His unit was surrounded and nearly wiped out. He was hit in the arm. It was shattered. He fell and lay in the field for hours. He lost a lot of blood. A Prussian doctor amputated his arm and treated his leg for a sword wound. Now they are saying he was a coward, had led his troops in surrender. A fabrication. He had no troops left to surrender, Josef. He was wounded and lying in the field. This is all made up."

"Scapegoats. The generals need scapegoats. Where is he?"

"I don't know. The soldiers said nothing. They just took him."

The military trial two months later lasted three days. Franz was acquitted. The army attorney assigned to his defense managed to find three witnesses of the unsuccessful cavalry charge at Koniggratz. All three testified that the commanding officer of the cavalry unit, Colonel Franz Schropfer, led the charge and had fought gallantly. Under questioning from the attorney, all three confirmed there was no supporting fire from infantry or artillery. The unit did not retreat, nor did it surrender. It was simply obliterated, in the words of one of the witnesses, an officer in the infantry who was close to what happened and had himself been taken prisoner following the battle.

Franz emerged from the trial, with his injuries and his honor vilified though vindicated in the end, a physically broken man. Disabled, he could no longer serve in the cavalry or anywhere else in the army. Despite his acquittal, the public knew of him as a traitor, a coward. The reputation followed him. Members of his family were affected as well, including Josef, identified in a newspaper as an important manager at the biggest bank of the empire. Through a friend and military college classmate, Franz was offered a teaching job at a military academy in Salzburg. He would teach military history to young cadets. Despite the acquittal, his loyal service and that of his father, he would never receive an apology nor a pension from the army.

One day Josef received word that Franz had died. Blood poisoning, according to Lizbeth, who had come to see Josef. "It happened so suddenly, Josef. He started retching one afternoon. Throwing up. Blood. We went to the hospital attached to the academy. He became delirious in the evening. By midnight, he was gone."

"My God. He didn't deserve this fate."

"He was weak. The war, the accusation, the humiliation. He never overcame it. His spirit was crushed. They did it to him."

"I am so sorry, Lizzy." He put his arms around her and held her for a long moment.

"Thank you, Josef. You have been so good to me."

"The funeral. When will it be? And where?"

"Two days from now, here in Vienna."

"What will you do now? You won't stay in Salzburg, will you?"

"No, it is not my place. I will go home. To Prague. My family is there. You know, Josef, I had just finished the tapestry. The portrait of him after the war. It was a better portrait of him than the reality. I don't want it now, though. You can have it, if you want it, along with the first one. I can't bear the memory. I have others I made of him. But not in uniform. You can have the two."

"Thank you, Lizbeth. If you wish, I will take them. Franz was my savior from drudgery. I will always be grateful to him. I will have something that I can remember him by."

"I have them with me. They are yours." She went to the entry way to the house and returned with the rolled-up paintings.

"Very well, my dear. I will take good care of them."

Chapter 3

A year later...

Josef arrived home. Rosa could see something was amiss. "What is it, my love? You look distressed."

"I am. Trouble coming. Bismarck, that wicked man, has decreed that Prussia will no longer have silver as the basis of its currency. There is fear that other nations will follow. This will be trouble for the bank, and trouble for me."

The trouble happened. His bank, the largest in the Empire and the only one operating in all the major cities of the realm, was over-exposed in silver. Its holdings were losing value daily. Depositors were withdrawing funds. If it went on for too long, the bank would fail. In the meantime, the war scandal and his cousin's troubles, even though he had been acquitted, had placed Josef's tenure at the bank in some jeopardy. Josef had learned that the prosecutor who lost the case was the brother of the senior managing director of the bank. The prosecutor's reputation was tarnished, ergo his family's as well. Anyone associated with Captain Franz Schropfer could expect to bear the burden of that, in one way or another. The elite of Vienna were that way. The principal managers of the bank all knew the relationship of Herr Tauer with the discredited cavalry officer.

In early 1868, the bank brought in a man to assume direction of the currency management section of the bank. The managing director who had hired Josef was protecting his position, establishing some distance. Herr Tauer was relegated to what was essentially a clerk's position.

"Do we go back to Bohemia, Josef?" asked Rosaline one evening.

"What is there to go back to? Working on the farm, for Schiffen? No, I will not. He would humiliate me. 'Herr Tauer, you want your job back? Someone else has it. I can put you in charge of the stables, the ones with the cattle. Sorry, Tauer.' No, Rosa, I will not do that. We will do something else."

"America. Why not America? Many other people are doing it," she said.

"I have thought of it. Maybe. We will need to save our money. That will be harder. My salary has been reduced. They only keep me because of what I know. Once the new people learn what I know, I will be sacked. I know it."

"We should prepare for America, Josef. My father, mother, Mary and Anna would come with us. We could start a business, acquire some land, and continue our family, but in America."

"We will need money, Rosa. We will need to save as much as we can. It may be the best solution for us, even if I am no longer a young man. I am almost forty. But yes, America could be good for us. I think you may be right."

Within a few months, Josef was no longer working at the bank. He was terminated. "Silver is not so important anymore, Tauer. You will have to find other work." He had seen it coming. "I am not surprised, Rosa. It was inevitable," Josef said to his wife that evening. Within a few weeks, he was hired by an import-export firm owned by a Jewish family. To be the bookkeeper. The salary was barely half of what he had been earning at the bank. "Rosa, we will go to America. But it will take some time. Tell no one we intend to do that. The Jew will fire me if he finds out."

Rosa's family returned to Ronsperg. Herr Spiess, her father, was welcomed back by the von Schiffen patriarch and given the job of looking after the cattle barn. "Just like I would have been," said Josef when he learned of it.

Josef worked hard for the business in Vienna. He needed to. The future depended on it. Survival as well. After a year with the firm, he moved on from bookkeeping to being in charge of working with Austrian companies for the supply of goods for export. It was at a higher salary as well, important for the move to America. While working for the firm and putting money aside, he and Rosaline and her parents managed to keep to themselves the secret of their plan.

It would take almost four years for it to happen. It would be the great Krach of Vienna that would ultimately do it for them.

In the meantime, in 1870, a new addition to the family came. A little girl. Barbara was the name they gave her.

"The Krach, Tauer. The Krach. No one has any money to buy our goods anymore." Six months after the Vienna stock market crashed in May 1873, bringing many of the biggest enterprises of the country down with it, the difficulties had trickled down to the suppliers and buyers of goods. Goods that Tauer's employer had bought, bartered and sold for over a hundred years. Companies and businesses large and small were failing everywhere in the Empire. The troubles had spread to other parts of Europe and beyond. The great European depression of the 1870's was on.

Josef and Rosaline were lingering at the dinner table. George had taken his sister to the parlor to read to her before bedtime. "We must leave, Rosa. There is nothing here. The business

28

is failing. Herr Levinson practically said so today. I will soon be out of work. I know it. We do not have all the money we wanted to have for America, but we have enough to get there and start something."

"Well, then, let's do it. Others in the family will want to do it as well, I am sure. Things are bad everywhere. Poppa and Momma will still want to come with us."

Josef hugged his wife. "We must get word to your parents. I will see what I can find for passage to New York. I must know how many of the family will be coming with us."

"What will we do there, Josef?" asked Rosaline

"I don't know, my dear. Farming maybe, but I don't know what land costs there. We could buy land somewhere. Land on the frontier is said to be plentiful. Maybe there are no more problems with the Indians. They all talk about that here, but maybe it is less of a danger. I don't know. I am getting older for farming. George could help on a farm, but he has not worked in that. Your father could help. He is in good health. But we must leave. We will be very poor and soon if we stay. We will see what we do when we get there."

Josef and Rosaline Tauer, their son George, 16, and daughter, Barbara, 4, along with Rosaline's father Anton Spiess, his wife Dorothea and their daughters Mary and Anna, 22 and 18 years old, and Johann Schropfer, 24, brother of cousin Franz, arrived in New York from Liverpool on the steamer US Idaho on May 1, 1874. "Hello to the great America!" exclaimed Josef as the ship made its way through the harbor. "A new day for us, Rosa. A new day. A new life."

Chapter 4

"Where do we go?" asked Josef at the bottom of the ramp in his heavily accented English.

"Over there," said the man in uniform. "There are papers to fill out. Someone will ask you questions. You see the line. You must go there. I see you speak English. It will help. There is a doctor as well. You and your family must be checked before you can leave."

"It is a long line."

"Yes, there are many people. Three ships today."

"After, where do we go? Where do we find lodging?"

"When you are finished with the papers and the medical examination, there will be someone who can help you. Someone who speaks German, although you do speak English. He can take you to a place where you can stay, at least for awhile."

"Someone who speaks German, you say," said Josef.

"Yes. There are Italians here for people from Italy. Irish for people from Ireland. Dutch for people from Holland. You are German."

"Austrian. But we speak German."

"You will see someone with a sign saying 'Deutsch'. Look for it. There will be more than one. One of the ships today came from Hamburg."

Four hours later, the family emerged and walked outside to the streets of teeming, bustling New York. They had certificates of arrival. Their official immigration papers would be available in a few days. Josef and his family looked around. People were everywhere. Old men, young men, boys. Shouting, jostling, hawking goods, offering whatever they had – food, clothes, shoes. "Hey, you!" a boy shouted at Josef. "You need to feed your family. I have everything for that! Cheese, sausage, apples, everything cheap!" Josef then saw a man with the sign 'Deutsch'. Their eyes met. The man came over to Josef. "You are German, sir," the man said in German. "No. Austrian, but we speak German of course," responded Josef.

"Very well. My name is Weiss. I help people like you settle in New York." The man's dialect and pronunciation were different from what Josef was used to.

"Very good. We need help. First, a place to stay. At least for awhile. Can you help us with that? There are nine of us," said Josef in German. "Where are you from?"

"Bremen. I have been here for five years. I work for the immigration authorities, helping people like you get started in America. Welcome."

"Thank you," responded Josef.

"For lodging, there is a kind man who has a house you could stay at – at least for awhile. It is especially for German speaking people. There are rooms with beds. It is acceptable in my view. People share a kitchen; you will perhaps find people with similar tastes, like in Germany. You will see. Eventually, where do you want to go?"

"What do you mean?" asked Josef.

"I mean in America, New York? Here? The West? Somewhere else?"

"We don't know yet. I have heard of St. Louis. Maybe find land starting in St. Louis. Or somewhere else. I have heard there are people from Austria who have gone to a place called Cincinnati."

The German took Josef by the elbow and motioned for the family to follow him. "We will go to the house. Come along, everyone."

As they walked, the man continued the discussion about destination. "There is Kansas, and there is Nebraska as well. It is farther than St. Louis or Cincinnati but there are many Germans and Czechs who have gone there. Mostly Catholics. There is much land available there. The Dutch go to Ohio and Pennsylvania, Italians stay here or go to New Jersey across the river."

Josef and his family were amazed at the activity of New York. Always someone selling something. Construction going on everywhere. Rosaline with little Barbara holding her hand as they followed Josef and the man named Weiss, were almost run over by a horse drawn delivery wagon careening down the street. "Get out of the way! Damn immigrants, look where you're going!" yelled the driver as he sped past a terrified Barbara and her mother.

"Look out, Madame!" said Weiss in German to Rosaline. "One must be extra careful on these streets. People are always in a hurry. You have to beware."

"I see. The house. Is it far?" responded Rosaline.

"No. Just a little bit further. We must go faster. I have to return to help other people."

"Rosa, where is the pouch? I can't find it."

"What pouch, Josef?"

"The one with the money. It was in the chest yesterday, hidden at the bottom. The chest was locked. I just checked the chest. Locked like it was yesterday, but the pouch is not there."

"Oh, no. It is all of our money." She could feel the panic. It was what she had always feared about America. "It is all of it, Josef! All of it!"

"Listen to me! Calm down! We must think about what happened! Everyone went downstairs at the same time as us. Johann, he was down there as well."

"Yes, everyone was there. Josef! I can't take this! It is all of our money! What are we going to do?"

"Shut up, Rosa! Stop the hysterics! We must think. We have to find the money, the person who did this. Crying will not help! What did you see? Who was in the room yesterday? Who came in? Where is your father, your mother? They may have seen someone, someone strange."

"Someone must have come in the room after we left, saw the chest, opened the lock somehow, took the pouch, then closed and locked the chest. It is the only explanation."

"You were supposed to bring it to a bank! You left it here! It was so stupid! Look what you have done! We are poor now, stuck in America with no money!" Tears were streaming down Rosaline's face.

"Open up a bank account for four days, Rosa? We are taking the train for St.Louis next week."

"No, we are not. We don't have the money because of you."
Rosaline pounded on Josef's chest. He grabbed her wrists.

"Rosa, we will make it."

"What will I tell my father and mother, my sisters?! The money was for their future as well as ours."

Josef never found out who took the money. The loss caused a rift with Rosa's parents. Neither of them spoke any English. They had not been robbed but they had little money to begin with when they arrived. Rosa's father did not say a word to Josef for over three weeks. The same with Rosa's sisters. But there was no going back. They had no money to go back. It would be three years before they left New York.

Josef had to find employment. The other men as well. Going on to Missouri or Kansas or anywhere else would have to wait. Within three days, he had found a job in a German brewery, loading barrels of beer on to wagons. Exhausting work. It was what was available. George found work delivering newspapers for one of the city's newspapers in the afternoon while spending mornings learning carpentry as an apprentice with a carpenter not far from where they lived. Rosa's father and Josef's cousin Johann had to find work as well. They caught on with a work crew excavating for the construction of new buildings in the city. English was not required. Rosaline found work as a seamstress in a local factory and her sisters as chambermaids in one of New York's many hotels.

Three years later, Josef Tauer and his extended family were still in New York. He was working at the brewery, but now as a bookkeeper and continuing to search for a way out of New York. Not enough money. It always came to that. The family was back on speaking terms, but life was rough. They lived in a cramped tenement above a store in Soho. Four rooms for the whole family. Life revolved around what went on in the street. George was regularly in fights which usually started with taunts about his accent. Little Barbara, starting when she was old enough to go school, became adapt at fighting boys. Italian, Polish, Jewish, Irish - boys who would pull her pigtails or laugh about her chubbiness. At six she learned to use her fists and soon was known to be the toughest little girl on Huston Street. One day she smacked a boy who was taunting her. Knocked him down after he pulled her pigtails. Other kids were watching. "Ok, next! Anybody else want a fist?" she said in the English she had learned on the street. From that day forward, anybody who picked on Barbara Tauer would get a surprise. All the other little girls in the neighborhood wanted to be friends with Barbara. They could count on her to fend off the boys. She became very popular.

Josef was constantly on the lookout for a way out. Money was always the problem. He met a man from Germany one day who said he was in the dry goods business. They had been introduced by a common acquaintance. The man had said he had family who had gone to Kansas and they were doing fine. The two had seen each other a couple of times and exchanged pleasantries. One day after work, Josef saw the man at the coffeehouse and suggested they have a beer together. He wanted to know about the family that had gone to Kansas. Soon Josef was saying he was looking for a way out of New York. "Away from the craziness of this place, out West, own some land and perhaps farm or otherwise build a better future for my family. When we first met, you told me about a brother who had gone to Kansas."

"Yes, he went there five years ago and is doing well. He now owns a general store in a town there. The town is Wamego, in the eastern part of the state. It is apparently in the midst of very good farm country, but vastly unsettled. He writes to me. We have been close as brothers. I want to go see him and I may move there myself. It may be an option for you. He tells me the government is encouraging people to settle there. Plenty of land available."

Josef had heard that before. "I know. I have heard it many times. My problem is having enough money to buy land and at the same time support my family. There are nine of us."

"Herr Tauer, you may be able to do it without a lot of money. You may not even have to buy land to start off."

"What do you mean? I can't have land if I don't buy it. I would rent it, I suppose."

"Hear what I have to say. What my brother told me. The railroads own a lot of land. They have vast tracts in the West they are now offering to people to occupy them, farm them. He says the railroads were not charging rent for these pieces of land. Basically, they are saying 'come bring your family and use our land. Farm it for as long as you want. We will charge you no rent. And you can eventually buy the land for a price we set in advance'. This could perhaps be a solution for you."

"No rent. This is good land? Good for farming and no rent?" asked Josef.

"That is what my brother tells me. The government just wants people to be on the land, working it, farming it. So do the railroads. People can buy the land later, he says, to make it their own. Something more about it, Tauer. The railroads agree to supply the wood to build the houses. One just has to provide the manpower to build them. This is all going on now."

Josef thought that this was something he could take advantage of. It would get them out of New York.

"So, Tauer, this may be an opportunity for you. My brother says there are many Germans and Czechs in his area; many people from Bohemia, apparently, with everyone pitching in to help new arrivals build their homes, get started. As well, he said most of the immigrants there were Catholic. You are Catholic, are you not?"

"Yes, we are Catholic. This is very interesting. This all helps your brother, I am sure. More Germans and Bohemians going there; good for his business, I suppose."

"Of course it could be good for his business. But nobody has to buy from him. I am just telling you of an opportunity, Tauer. You should try to find out for yourself."

The next day, Josef received permission to take the afternoon off and went to the immigration office to enquire about the railroad land offer in Kansas. "It is true, sir. The Union Pacific Railway wants people to occupy the company's land. They will either sell it to anyone who wants to buy it to farm or rent it to people who cannot afford to buy, but perhaps could in time, at no cost in the meantime. And yes, the railroad will supply the materials for the houses on the land. An agreement with the government. The railroads have been given the rights to the land but they must make it available for settlement. Here is a sheet of information on the offer. Many immigrants are taking advantage of it." The man told Josef the program was relatively new. Not many immigrants knew about it, he said, but with its success so far, it would be promoted more.

"Thank you, sir. If I want to take advantage of this, how would I do it?" asked Josef.

"Union Pacific has an office down the street. Here is the address. Go see them. They will probably tell you to get to St. Louis or Kansas City to learn more about what specific plots of land are available. You will probably have to go out there. But there are government agents in Kansas who can help you. I can give you a list of the offices for that. Wait a moment. I will get that for you. You will need to pay for your passage out there, however."

"Thank you. You have been very kind." Josef left and walked to the railroad office down the street.

Later that evening, he told Rosaline about the program. "We will be able to acquire land in Kansas from the railroad, Rosa. We must do this. I see no other way."

Chapter 5

BARBARA

We left New York when I was eight years old. I remember the train ride. It was long, so long. We lived in Wamego for awhile, in a big house where everyone spoke German, just like Momma. Daddy - we call him that now, but before coming to Kansas, he was always Poppa - spoke English to most everyone except Momma and grandfather and grandmother and so did George. My big brother who looked after me. I miss him now, but he has his own family.

After a time with the German family who had the store in Wamego, we moved into our house in the country. I was nine years old then. It was two hours by wagon from town. He and the other men had to go there every day to build it and sometimes stayed for days at a time until they ran out of food. The house they built was a big one and smelled of wood. It smelled of wood for a long time. I will always remember it. It was at the edge of a large field of tall grass not far from a creek and a line of trees. Daddy and George, grandfather and Johann, had all worked building it and were so proud. George had learned to be a carpenter in New York and this allowed the men to finish the house quickly. Johann, who joined us in Kansas, had left New York six months after arriving, going to St. Louis, where he worked as a deckhand on a riverboat, then found work in construction. This helped in the building of the house and the barns that would come later.

One day, not long after they started to build the house, Daddy took me with him. There were piles of wood everywhere. George told me the railway had provided all the wood as well as the plans for the house. The houses were all the same. I remember that. The family over the hill behind us had a house just like ours. There were German-speaking men who helped Daddy and the other men build it. One was so taken with my aunt Mary, who was a beautiful woman and had turned down suitors in New York, that he proposed marriage one day. The young man was handsome and his father had a prosperous livery stable and blacksmith shop in Wamego. Anna, who was also pretty, would have suitors continually coming to the house in the country and married one within a year of moving there with the rest of us.

Daddy became a farmer again. He was not used to it. It was difficult at the start, but he had George, Johann and my grandfather to help him. It seemed I could run forever in any direction from that house. There was a little school two miles down the road. It was a lot different from the one in New York. There were only fourteen children in the whole school at different grades. I would hear everything the older children were learning. I learned a lot very fast. The first year, Daddy or Johann or George would take me in the wagon we had, but later when I was older, I would walk it with the two boys who lived nearby. Momma worried about Indians. So did Daddy although no Indians had attacked anyone in eastern Kansas for over ten years, according to Sam Becker, the sheriff who would come to the house from time to time to have schnapps with Daddy. "Your great German tradition, Tauer," he would say. Momma often did not let me walk to school. So I missed a lot of days. I passed my school years anyway. People told me I was smart. We stayed in that house for four years.

Then we moved again. Daddy told me then that the new house was ours. We owned it. I did not know what that meant or why that was so important, that we had to move. I liked it where we were. I of course know the importance of that now. A few years later, I remember Daddy saying he could have bought the land where we had been, but found something better, with more trees and better land for growing corn and wheat, and for grazing animals. He and George and Johann and grandfather and many other men Daddy knew came to help build the new house that had a stone foundation and a well right next to the house. We had a well where we were before, but it would run dry in the summer and we would have to take water from the creek. It was often dirty and had to be boiled before we could drink it. Daddy had a pump next to the new house and soon a windmill that pumped water into a big tank. That allowed us to have more animals. A Czech family quickly took over the house where we had lived.

I was thirteen when we moved. By that time, there was a high school in the village, next to the church. Daddy or George would take me there in the wagon, along with a boy who lived down the road. The boy, who was a year older than me, was my protector. That's what he told everyone at school, although it wasn't really needed. But Momma liked to hear that as she was always afraid of the Indians, whose reservation was not far away. The boundary of the reserve was just over the hills behind our land. We never had a problem in those days, but Momma was afraid anyway.

I also had the first of my two baby sisters by that time – Maggie. There was a baby born two years after we arrived in Kansas, but he died soon after birth. It was just like the three others who had died before – two before I was born and a third when we were in New York. Momma had trouble having babies. Maggie was healthy though and was two years old when we moved to the new house. At ten, I was so happy to have a baby sister. I looked after her all the time. When Maggie was two and three years old, she would wait for me on the porch of the house every day when I came home from school, seeing me walk over the hill and then running to greet me. She would sometimes trip and fall down and scrape her knees, but then get up and keep running until she reached me. She would hold back her tears as she didn't want me to see her cry. I would pick her up and we would walk to the house and I would wash her knees and give her a cookie and a glass of milk. I remember all of that as if it were yesterday. Maggie is now eleven, far prettier than I and looking after Louise, the baby of the family.

I was never pretty like Maggie. George always teased me about being chubby. *Mollig* was the German word he would use. I hated him saying that. Just like what boys would say about me in New York. Momma said I had the German build. Strong. Built to work hard, she said, like her cousins and aunts back in Bohemia. Because of that, none of the boys at the school took much interest in me. I didn't really care, although I did down deep inside. I made sure I stayed at the top of the class. To hell with them. In any case, by the time I was sixteen, I was anxious to leave the farm and the little community where we were, although I was sad about leaving Momma and Poppa. Poppa was fifty-six years old when I left. Momma was forty-eight. Fortunately, George and Johann were around as well as my grandfather, who was still robust enough to look after the animals – two workhorses, another one for riding, four cows, usually four to eight heifers and steers and ten pigs, sometimes growing to fifteen or twenty, and always two or three dozen chickens. Daddy, with the help of Johann, had bought another half section of land next to ours. Both George and Johann, who had their own families by the time I left, built houses on that land and with Daddy, they managed the farm that had grown to over 600 acres. In time, the small herds of beef cattle and pigs would grow and be the basis for the income of the farm. The Tauers would be in the meat business – meat on the hoof.

I went to Topeka when I finished school. There was a German family there Daddy had known since we first came to Kansas. They were happy to take me in. They had a large house and

I felt part of the family. I soon found a job working as a clerk in the state land office. I was happy to leave the country. Topeka was the city, as exciting as city life could be in Kansas, although not nearly as exciting as New York. Although it had been over ten years since we had left New York, I remembered very well its hustle and bustle. But Topeka was just fine. There was a theatre on Main Street and I went to see every production that came to town. Sometimes I would take Maggie with me, when I could bring her to Topeka. There were parks and sandbars on the river running through town where people could go, have picnics and have fun. I would often go back to the farm when I could, on weekends and at holidays - Easter, the 4th of July, Thanksgiving, Christmas. There was a train to Wamego and George would pick me up in the wagon at the depot on Saturday mornings and bring me back on Sunday afternoons to take the train back.

By the time I was sixteen, little Louise, the baby of the family, was two years old. Maggie was four when Louise was born. The two of them are close. They are always doing things together, even if they are four years apart. They are also the ones I am sure will look after Mom and Dad when they grew old. In a way, I was lucky to be able to leave home when I did. I was the big sister who had an important job and who would do great things, said Daddy to friends and others he would see at church on Sundays. When I was eighteen, I met a boy in Topeka and fell head over heels in love. His sister worked in the same office as I and suggested to him one day that he invite me to accompany him to a picnic with other young people at Lake Shawnee, not far from town. We had a great time that day and I quickly fell for him. He was Irish and his name was Hugh. He was tall with dark eyes and beautiful wavy brown hair. He was lovely. I was smitten. He was my first real beau and after we spent a few afternoons together that summer, he said he wanted to marry me. He said he would only propose to me when he could afford to support a wife, although I told him he would not have to support me. I was capable of working and earning my keep. "No, we will do it my way. We will marry when I can support you," he would say. We would see each other regularly, hold hands and kiss when my chaperone wasn't looking. But tragedy struck. Hugh drowned. He dove off of one of the small cliffs at the end of the lake and never came up. They found his body hours later. He had invited me to go with him and his sister to the picnic that day, but I could not go. I had agreed to go home for the weekend. It was Hugh's best friend who came to the house on Sunday night to tell me. I was distraught for weeks afterward. I went to dances with other young men after that, but no one came close to being what Hugh had been. I thought I would end up a spinster. Maybe I will.

I have always been fascinated by the circus. When we were still in New York, when I was a little girl, my father took me to the circus that was playing. Elephants, tigers, clowns, magnificent white horses, all doing tricks. Dancing elephants. Tigers leaping through rings. It was all so exciting. I never forgot it. When I saw the notice in the newspaper for the job in Topeka, I could not resist applying for it. I started working for the Barnett and Wilson Circus as a helper. After a few days, the owner, the widow of the founder who had died two years before, offered me to become her travelling secretary, to replace the one who had left. The job meant following her and the circus everywhere. It was different from anything I expected to be doing. I accepted. I loved it then and I still do.

Chapter 6

MAGGIE

"Barbara, why are you leaving? I don't want you to go."

Maggie, the feisty, energetic, adventuresome little girl who adored her older sister, was distraught. "Maggie, I am going to Topeka, to work, find a job. You will look after Louise now. It's your turn, and I will come back often. Topeka is not far. You can even come and visit me."

Maggie would become the new big sister. She formed a bond with her little sister. Louise would run up the hill to greet her sister just like Maggie had done with Barbara, would stumble and scrape her knees, and Maggie would take care of them. In her twenties, Louise would joke about the scars.

Maggie would also be the Tauer who befriended the Indians. When she was eight and up on the hill behind the house one day, she saw a boy halfway down the other side. The boy turned. She waved. He waved back. She started down the hill to see who it could be. The boy was dark-skinned, about as tall as her. Indian. From over there. I will go down, she thought. Maybe I can make a friend. If he tries to hurt me, I will scream. George is in the field. He will hear me. Mother always panics when we talk about the Indians. Maybe they are not so bad.

She approached the boy, who was shy and recoiled a bit as Maggie came close. "Hello, I am Maggie. Who are you?" The boy remained silent. "Hello again. Can you talk? What is your name?"

"I can talk. My name is Beshno. It means Bald Eagle."

The two would become friends and the friendship would last with the boy and later his family, for as long as Maggie lived in the country and later under other circumstances. Rosaline would have been aghast at Maggie's relationship with an Indian child, as would her father, which they would eventually demonstrate when they found out. Maggie remembered the times when she was five or six when Daddy would talk about catching Indian boys who would be stealing a chicken or two in the years when she was a baby. George once told her that their father would put the boys in the wagon with George or Johann holding them and bring them to the gate of the reservation. He did not want to report them to the sheriff. "It would only cause worse trouble, Rosa," George remembered Daddy saying. "They are only young boys. I don't want older boys or men or whatever coming over and causing us trouble if we report them."

One day on the hill behind their property, Maggie met Beshno's sister Kewanee, which meant Prairie Hen, and their mother. They invited her to come to their hut on the reservation, to share with them the rabbit they had caught that morning. She accepted and made it back home before anybody became worried about where she was. She managed to keep the friendship a secret for close to three years. Every few weeks, she would go up the hill in early afternoon when school was out and sometimes see Beshno in the distance. They would wave and meet at the bottom of the hill, race across the little valley down below to see who was fastest – Maggie sometimes won. They would chase a rabbit, climb one of the cottonwoods at the bottom, pick some wildflowers and see who had the prettiest ones, and they would talk. Once, Maggie went with Beshno to the reservation and their hut and his father told Maggie about how the Pottawatomie got where they were. At the end of the story, the afternoon was almost over and Maggie had to run back. But she had been told about the long march from Indiana, all the people who died along the way, their origins in what was now Michigan and Canada, and the loss of their lands in all of those places. She learned that they had more land when they first came to the territory, fifty years before, including the land of the Tauer farm that they lost when President Grant gave in to demands for more land for the settlers. One evening at supper when she was eleven, Josef was talking about the Indians over the hill. "They are savages. They steal and lie. They could erupt any time and start scalping people again. It has only been a few years since the last Indian uprising. They steal our chickens, they could steal our horses and cattle and much more."

"Daddy, you are wrong," said Maggie. Everybody was stunned. The girl had never spoken like that to her father. George, Johann, Rosaline, Josef, grandpa and grandma Anton and Dorothea, Louise who was seven and had kept Maggie's secret for so long, looked at Maggie.

"What? Maggie, what are you saying?"

"I am saying they are not savages. They are very kind. They are just poor and they don't like us because of what we have done to them."

"How do you know that? Is that what that schoolteacher from St. Louis at the school now tells you?"

"No, Daddy. It comes from the people themselves. You must know now that I have been to the reservation over the hill. I have a friend. He is very nice. We run together. I know his sister, his mother and father. I know the story of them and how they got here. We are sitting on land that was theirs."

"What?" Rosaline was aghast. George was the next to pipe in. "It can't be, Maggie. They will hurt you. It will happen. What are you doing?" Josef was speechless. He looked at his daughter. Words would not come out. Maggie and Louise shared a glance. Louise grimaced. She knew and had kept quiet. She knew that Maggie would be punished. Nobody said anything for a moment. George was the first to say anything. "All those times you went over the hill and you would come back with wildflowers in your hands. You were seeing the Indian. What did he do to you?"

"He did nothing, George. We played, we ran, we chased rabbits, even deer one day. Nothing happened to me."

"Maggie, you will no longer be allowed to go over the hill. I will not have it," said Josef in German.

"Well, I'm going to do it anyway sometime and you won't be able to stop me, because you won't even see me. They are friends now and you have nothing to worry about."

Maggie also made friends with another boy from the land next to the Tauer farm. Billy Knecht was a year older than her. The two of them would walk to school together and later in high school would ride in Billy's father's wagon or ride their fathers' horses to school. Billy was taken with Maggie, who was vivacious, pretty, witty and mischievous. She would break out laughing or say something that others around would laugh at. She was the most lively and popular girl in the school. For Maggie, Billy was the tall, handsome boy who was smart, and whose family had the most beautiful and fastest horses in the county. Billy knew about Maggie's friendships amongst the Indians but refrained from criticizing her for it. He had once, soon after they had started high school, saying she was an Indian lover and kisser of savages in front of others at school and Maggie went to him and slapped him so hard, he almost fell down. Maggie turned to everyone and then said, "If anybody else has a nasty remark about me and my Indian friends, tell it to me now and I will hit you just as hard. I don't kiss Indians. I just happen to respect them. Ok? Anybody else?" Johann, who had picked up colorful terms about people while working on the Mississippi river boats years before, made the comment when he heard about the encounter, "Maggie is our own tough little broad." Billy would never again say a negative word to Maggie about Indians.

Chapter 7

Boston, September 1896

It had been a long trip, thought Barbara. The voyage from Liverpool had kindled faint memories of the trip to America when she was a little girl. That terrible journey on the ship with those big sails and the big waves with Momma sick and throwing up every day. She was probably pregnant. Grandma and Mary and Anna sick as well. Why weren't the men sick? Anyway, this time, it was a steamship and it didn't rock like that one with the sails.

But Europe. So different from what I thought it would be. Paris, Rome, Milan, Copenhagen, London. So different from what Daddy had told us - war, mean, pompous counts and barons, about being poor landless peasants while the rich dined and drank and kept everyone else in servitude. The village where no one could own land except the count was not what I saw. Glorious cities, with prosperity everywhere. Neat little villages in the countryside. Ruth calls it The Golden Age. I could love living in Europe. I don't think I will ever say that to Daddy, though. He would be very upset. So would Momma. In any case, I would need a husband and that is not happening. Edward who was so intent on following me around after Chicago, professing his love, went off somewhere after coming to see me. Disappeared. Probably got tired of trying to follow me around. It did not make much sense. It was never really clear where he was from to begin with, and he probably would never want to live in Europe anyway. Getting to be an old maid. I already am! That is my condition. I must slim down as I am not as attractive as I could be. My German build, says Momma. In any case I am not long enough in any one place to develop a relationship. And there is no one in the circus who I would dare want to spend my life with.

Barbara looked over towards the ladies who were into what appeared to be heavy gossip. A young couple sat down at the table around the edge of the fountain. A waiter came. She ordered an iced tea. She went back to her thoughts. How much longer do I stay with this? Mrs. Barnett pays me well. She is a wonderful boss. She lets me go home for a month every year. I have money in the bank. I help at home with it. Sent some for Maggie to go to the convent school in Leavenworth. She turned it down, impetuous girl. Wants to remain close to home – and to Billy, that big lug who has captured her heart. Louise could do it, go to the convent school instead of Maggie and get some real education, but Momma wants her to stay on the farm. Says she is too vulnerable, too impressionable. I need her here, she said in the letter, written in her rough English. Anna must have helped her with it. Poppa is getting old. Grandpa and grandma are close to ninety. Maggie will leave soon, too independent to accept to stay around for very long. Only as long as Billy is still around. They say he is going to Wamego to finish high school. Barbara's thoughts turned back to her own situation.

I will have to stay. Mrs. Barnett is good to me, and I see the world. I meet important people. Last evening, the Governor of Massachusetts. In Copenhagen, the Crown Prince. Nine governors I have met now in the last two years, and countless mayors. Not bad for a simple girl from Pottawatomie County. In time, I will certainly have enough money to start a business, open a shop in Kansas City or Topeka. The fashions of Europe in the heart of America. Maybe an acceptable man will come along after all.

Mrs. Barnett thinks I am not only her secretary but also a good ambassador for the circus. We work well together. I'll stay.

Chapter 8

February 1897....

"You had the chance to go to Leavenworth, Maggie," said Josef as the family was finishing Sunday dinner. "You are the best one for that. But no, you wanted to stay here. All because of Billy. You are going to leave anyway, which will leave Momma with no one to help her if Louise goes to that school."

"You are preventing LouLou from getting ahead, Daddy. If she stays here, she will be stuck here."

"She's a beautiful, intelligent girl, she will find a husband around here."

"Not if you and Momma are still living, Daddy. You won't let her. You don't let her go anywhere now. Boys are all around and ogle at Louise. Which should not be a bad thing. There was the Christmas dance at the school. You wouldn't let her go. She was humiliated. All her friends were there."

"Well, we have to protect her from that, from becoming a victim of her looks. The boys. They are mostly all too old for her. I have seen them at church. She is only thirteen. And it is the tradition. It has always been that way in the family. Youngest girl looks after the aging parents. That is that. I will not talk about it anymore."

Maggie and Louise were in their room. "Daddy is being unreasonable. He is being unfair to you. You should have the opportunity to go to Leavenworth. Barbara will pay for it. She has always said she would."

"You had the opportunity to go last year. Why didn't you? You're the smart one, Maggie."

"I didn't want to leave. I was already sixteen. I didn't want to leave here, because I knew if I did, I would never come back and would never marry Billy. That is what I want, Louise. I always have. Billy is starting a job with the bank in Wamego. I finish high school in May. I plan to find a job there. I will live with a family, one who will take me in. If I stay here, Daddy and I will argue all the time and he won't want to take me to work in Wamego. I can't live here and have a job in town."

"You're so funny, Maggie. You amaze me. Even the way you get the chickens for Momma, like you did this morning. Chasing them in the field, you always catch up to the one you want, then grabbing them by the neck, bringing them to the block, spinning them around, then chopping their head off, all so fast, then watching them run around with no head until they drop. So funny. I laugh every time you do it."

"Yeah, Momma never liked to do that. She would sometime miss a bit with the chop plus she didn't like to run after them. I did it once, then it was always me after that. 'Maggie, chicken time,' *huhn zeit,* she has always said in German, calling me Marghareta when she does it."

"Let's do something crazy, Maggie. Liven things up downstairs, change the mood. Mom and Dad need to laugh a bit," said Louise. "You're right. Let's do something. I have an idea," said Maggie. An hour later, Maggie and Louise came down the stairs to the parlor, where Josef was reading and Rosa was knitting. Louise had a monstrous lady's hat on her head with feathers protruding in all directions, with a large colored shawl wrapped around her, covering shoulders to knees, and had a pair of George's work boots on. Maggie had another hat on, one of her father's wide brimmed felt hats with chicken feathers tucked all around into the band. She wore one of Rosa's mid-length nightshirts with a red sash around her waist, three strings of fake pearls around her neck, a gift from Barbara in her travels, and a pair of riding boots. Their cheeks were painted with rouge powder, their lips with heavy red lipstick, both recent gifts from Barbara as well. They danced across the floor, kicking their legs in the air like the can can girls they had seen at the fair in Wamego, singing the song Yankee Doodle Dandy. "Yes, yes, yes", they screeched, "Yankee Doodle went to town, a-riding on a pony, he stuck a feather in his hat, and called it macaroni…Yankee Doodle, keep it up, Yankee Doodle dandy, Mind the music and the step and with the girls be handy!," all the while laughing in their hilarious costumes, smiling at their parents, who stared at their daughters, then broke out laughing as the girls danced from one side of the room to the other, kicking their legs in the air from side to side. The girls ended the show by putting an arm around each other and looking at their parents with grins on their faces and twinkles in their eyes. "Your daughters, for better or worse." Josef broke out with a big grin. Rosa had a hand over her mouth. Both were astounded. "We love you," said Josef. "Our amazing daughters. What do you need now?"

"Nothing, Daddy. We just needed to have fun. They don't do this in Bohemia, do they?" asked Maggie.

"No, they don't. A lot of fun from you two. I think we needed it."

That evening after dinner, Josef went outside to the porch and sat on the steps, observing the sunset with its hues of red and orange. He thought about his daughters. What a pair. Maggie, always getting dressed up in something crazy, putting on plays and skits. At school, and even with Kewanee. My God, on the reservation. The gunny sack race last week at the fair. Beat all the boys, hopping down the field in that sack in her bloomers, Rosa covering her face. Started the egg business. Convinced me to let her do it. To town every Saturday morning, with George and the wagon. Then the day when she decided she would not wait for him, harnessed the gelding, and went by herself. At fourteen. The egg business all hers now, no waiting on anybody. Raises the chicks, organizes the feed for them, does it all. She buys material for her mother with the money, and for her own clothes and costumes. The hat she had on this afternoon and the scarf – egg money. Kewanee and the Indians. Has got me with a different mind on all that. Over here often now, like part of the family. I never thought I would ever think something like that.

Louise, the sweet, innocent jewel of the family. Thirteen now, will be a beautiful woman. Maggie with the eggs and the chickens, Louise with her pet lambs and rabbits. And the young calves. They get bigger and we have to do something with them, but I would have hell to pay if we butchered them. Have to take them to market instead. Crisis every time. She's beyond that now, but still. The number one babysitter in the family. Told George, Johann, Mary and Anna to bring their kids here on Saturdays. A weekly break for the mothers. Sometimes all nine of them are here. Organizes different stuff for them every week – games in the house or outside, reads to them – all of them sitting with their legs crossed, listening intently. They love her. Will she be stuck here? No. We won't live forever. I just wish we didn't have to have these arguments.

Chapter 9

1899..

    Will Knecht, known as Billy to everyone in the country, graduated from high school in Wamego and soon after was hired by Willard Benson, his father's friend and the President of the Farmer's Bank, to work there as a clerk. The Knecht farm, adjacent to that of the Tauers on the other side from the reservation, was one of the largest and most prosperous in Pottawatomie County. Alfred Knecht was one of the first immigrants to buy land from the railroad in Kansas and because of that, had the choice of sections with the best pastures and water and took advantage of it. He raised horses and cattle. He had worked on contract for the Army in the 1870's, capturing wild horses in western Kansas, helped by other recently arrived immigrant men who he would hire. He would bring the horses back to his farm, break them, breed them, then sell them to the Army. This led to contracts for supplying beef as well. He often bought cattle ready for slaughter from Josef. The Knecht and Tauer cattle along with other cattle bought from other farmers would often be seen trudging down the road to the slaughterhouse in Wamego, with local boys acting as cowboys leading them along. Over the years, Alfred Knecht became one of the Farmer's Bank of Wamego's biggest customers. Will, as third son, would not inherit the farm or the livestock business. There were two brothers ahead of him. As the odd boy out, he would have to find something else. His father found it for him. "You're good with figures. I will propose you to my old friend at the bank. Who knows. You could maybe run the place some day."

A year after Will had been away and in town working, Maggie found a family in Wamego to take her in. The family needed someone to look after their young children and, in preparation for school, teach them to read and write. Maggie fit the bill. She was eighteen and happy to be on her own, although she returned regularly to the farm on weekends, all the while feeling indebted to Louise for taking over the care of their parents. She and Will saw each other regularly, chaperoned by the missus of the house where she lived, per the agreement with Josef and Rosaline.

"When are you going to propose to me, Will Knecht? I have been here for close to a year now, and you have not said anything about it. Well?"

"Maggie, you know that is going to happen. It has always been so."

"I suspect you are taking for granted that we will be married. Well, I am nineteen and of marrying age. Are you going to ask me or do I go back to the farm and find another husband? Or somebody else here in Wamego? There are a few young men around who seem to be very interested when I walk down the street."

"You have always been pretty direct. You know that it has always been the case that we will marry. We see each other all the time, although I am tired of being spied on by your mistress. I am saving money so we can be married and have our own home."

"You're always saying that."

Will looked at Maggie and knew it was about time he made the move he knew he would have to make… "Ok, Miss Margaret Tauer, will you marry me?"

"You will have to ask my father. You can do that on Sunday. But yes, I will marry you, unless my father somehow prevents me from doing it. It's about time, Will." She then turned to him, looked around to make sure no one was looking as they crossed the small park in front of the court house, reached up and kissed him on the cheek.

Chapter 10

LOUISE

Louise ran to the barn and found her father in the stable with one of the horses. It was mid-afternoon on a hot day. "Daddy, Momma has collapsed in the yard. I called out for her. She did not respond. I went outside and there she was on the ground. Unconscious. I tried to revive her, but got no response. I'm very, very worried, Daddy. She was not moving at all. We need to get the doctor."

"Oh, my God. Yes, I will have to get him. Or maybe George. Somebody. Was she breathing?"

"Yes, but unconscious."

Josef walked as quickly as he could to the house with Louise and saw his wife on the ground. He checked her pulse. "I will ride out to the pasture to get George to come back here and help us get Momma into the house. I will have him ride to the doctor's place. Stay with her here until we get back. I'll be back in ten minutes."

Rosaline "Rosa" Tauer died that night. The doctor said she had a stroke. She never regained consciousness. She was three weeks short of her 62nd birthday.

After the doctor had left, Josef was sitting on the steps of the porch. My God, what now? Rosaline, the love of my life, the anchor of the family. We've known each other since we were kids.

She was the little girl next door, who suddenly became a woman at fourteen, with me falling in love with her when I noticed. Through so much together. Eight babies. She wanted each one so bad. Our last embrace last night. I never thought it would be the last…….Here I am now, so far away from home. So, so far…..She will be with her mother and father, across from the church. I have my children. My God. They will have to do.

Louise stayed with her father and took care of him. She helped with the farm, working with George, Johann and his boys, expanding the hen house, selling eggs at the town market, just as Maggie had done. A year or so after Rosaline died, a young man came to the house. He was with a surveying crew working for the county, plotting new roads to accommodate the increasing numbers of newcomers. He had seen Louise at church and was taken with her. He said he was from Nebraska. He invited her to accompany him to the 4th of July picnic. They went and had a good time. Josef saw them, how they appeared to enjoy each other's company that day and waited for the question to come. The young man came to see Louise every chance he had after that while the crew was working in the area. One evening, he came calling. It was to see Josef. "I have come to see you, sir."

"Come in. I am not surprised," responded Josef. "I think I know why you are here."

The young man followed Josef to the parlor and sat down. "Sir, may I have the permission to ask your daughter to marry me? Will you allow me to do that, sir?"

"Young man, you can do that, assuming she wanted to marry you herself, but only as long as you come to live here with her. She will not leave the farm. Will you accept to do that?"

"Sir, Louise is the most wonderful girl I have ever met. She is certainly the loveliest, if I may say so. But living here. I don't know about that. She didn't tell me she had to stay here."

"She is only seventeen, the last one of my children, and will have to be close by. Actually, on the farm here. My wife, Louise's mother, is gone. There is no one else to take care of this home and I am getting old, although I won't live forever. If you are willing to become a farmer or agree to at least live on the farm here with us until I'm gone, I grant you permission to ask her. Have you discussed the idea of marriage with her?" asked Josef.

"I have. She said I would have to talk to you. She did not mention anything about the need for us to live here."

"When did you speak to her about this? She has said nothing to me."

"An hour ago. I have been here since then, sitting in the back, waiting for you to arrive. I told her at church yesterday I would come after work. It is all happening so fast, Mister Tauer. I am leaving here in five days."

"And you want to take Louise with you? In five days? Young man, you want to get married between now and then and then leave? With my daughter?"

"Er, yes sir. That's what this would mean. I guess it is not possible."

"You are right, it is not possible. I don't want you proposing marriage to my daughter. She's too young and she is not going anywhere. I'm sorry."

Chapter 11

Wamego, August 1903...

"She has lost the baby, Mr. Tauer." Will had ridden out to the farm in his buggy to inform the family. George was there with his wife Mary and their young boys, Albert and Leo, along with Louise.

"The second one now," said Josef. "What was it, a boy or a girl?"

"It was a boy."

"Lord God. Only one month to go. Like her mother. Rosa had similar problems. Our dear, lovable Maggie, will she be a mother someday?"

"Knowing Maggie, this will not be the end of her having children," said Louise.

"I think you're right. She's a tough girl," said Josef.

"We know where it comes from. From you." replied Louise.

"Let's all go see her. I'll hook up the horses."

"We are going to keep trying, Will. I will be a mother. It is what I have always wanted, and I don't care what the doctor says," said Maggie as the family left the house to return to the farm.

It would be another three years before Maggie was pregnant. This time, the pregnancy went all the way. A little girl, Frances, was born on Labor Day 1907, a fitting name for the day. Maggie's labor that day was long and arduous. But the little girl was healthy. Maggie was a mother.

In the meantime, Will Knecht had moved up at the bank. He had been promoted to senior teller and was on his way to being one of the principal managers at the bank, the biggest one in the county, serving Wamego and the nearby communities of Alma, St. George, Rossville and beyond. Four years after the birth of Frances and ten years into his marriage with Maggie, Will was made assistant cashier, one of the most prestigious positions in Wamego. He and Maggie bought a house up the hill from downtown at the corner of Elm and 5th Street. It was an area where the most prosperous merchants of the town lived, along with the judges, lawyers and doctors who served the area. Maggie was proud. Her man was important, and she had become one of the important ladies of Wamego. While raising her little Frances, she managed to continue doing some of the things she had enjoyed so much as a girl in the country. She started a theatre group that put on comedies twice a year. One in the spring, another in the fall. She also started a canasta club. Every Monday evening, twelve ladies would show up at the Knecht house to play canasta. Some of their husbands would come along and talk local politics while their ladies played cards. A big crowd with Maggie relishing it all. She was widely viewed as the most entertaining hostess in town. Life was good. But she was told she would never be able to have another child. Frances was it.

Chapter 12

1909.

"Barbara, I have had enough. I am selling the business."
Barbara and Ruth were in Philadelphia. Barbara was aware that her
boss had met someone the previous evening while the show was
on. Now she knew what it was about. "The Robinson Brothers
have made me an offer I cannot refuse. The price is more than
acceptable. We have much to discuss."

"I am not surprised, really. This came about last evening, I
suppose."

"Yes, it culminated last evening. Ed Robinson came to see
me in New York last month. I thought about it and last night said
yes. I am fifty-four years old and I want to enjoy the remaining
years of my life. I am going to Palm Beach and become what people
call a socialite. The new, much larger circus with all of their big cats
and clowns and acrobats to go along with our elephants, horses, fire
and sword eaters will be named the Robinson Brothers Barnett and
Wilson Circus. I am so relieved!"

"Very well. I am happy for you, Madame." Before she could
say anything else, the lady continued what she had to say.
"Knowing you now as well as I do, Barbara, I don't think you will
want to work for the Robinsons. So, I am going to take care of
you."

"You are right. I will not want to work for them," said Barbara.

"This is all happening very quickly, but I want to do something for you.......We were a good team of tough ladies in a man's business."

Barbara would be given enough money to start not one, but in the end, two businesses. The first one was a ladies fine clothing store, a millinery as they were called in those days, which she opened on Topeka's main street, with the second being something close to what she had always wanted to do, which was own a hotel with a fine restaurant. That something was an elegant rooming house in the city, catering to gentlemen who needed temporary lodging with excellent service and fine food and were willing to pay a premium for it. Within a year and a half of coming back to Topeka and opening the shop for ladies hats and clothing accessories which rapidly became quite successful, Barbara had bought a large house. It was not far from the shop and directly across the street from the state legislature and she converted it into what she had in mind. The house would become the preferred lodging for politicians from across the state while the legislature was in session as well as for businessmen visiting the city. It had twenty rooms on three stories along with a large parlor and dining area on the ground floor. There was a big veranda covering three sides of the house, with large wicker chairs and tables with waiter service. Soon, much of the state's business was said to be carried out on the veranda and in the dining room of Miss Tauer's boarding house. She charged more for the rooms than any other rooming house in the city, with meals that were reputed to be the best in Topeka - an elegant home away from home, a step up from the city's hotels, and it worked.

She also quickly paid off the remaining mortgages on the Tauer properties, relieving her aging father of the last burden he had taken on a few years earlier in his expansion of the cattle business. It was not a large burden, but one which she knew bothered her father. It came to a head one day, soon after Barbara's return to Kansas.

"Daddy, why don't you sell the farm? You are too old for this. You are almost 80, George is no longer interested in doing the farm work, and Johann's sons are not exactly the most energetic managers of the operations."

"Barbara, I am not going to sell this property. It is all we have in America. All that I have worked for. What would I do? Where would I go?"

"Go to Wamego. Maggie is there, so is George and his family. Louise is wasting her life here, looking after you. She's 26 years old, for God's sake. It's not fair to her."

"Does she complain? It is her duty. It is part of being in a family like ours."

"Yes, she complains. We all adore her, Daddy. She needs to get out of here. She has a life to live. In the meantime, George tells me the farm is losing money. Is that the case?" asked Barbara.

Josef looked at his daughter. He could try to hide it, but he decided not to. "Yes, it is losing money, I must admit. For the first time. Cattle prices are terrible. The surplus we had is being eaten up, I'm afraid. Feed, machinery, cattle selling at below cost. Will at the bank knows all about it."

"You took out the mortgage four years ago to buy all that cattle and it has not worked out."

"Worst thing I ever did, and almost as bad as the actual trouble, which is Will working at the bank and knowing pretty much everything about it. It means Maggie knows and I am sure

Louise does too, because they talk all the time. Now you know. George didn't have to tell you."

"Daddy, that mortgage is burning at you. Like you say, cattle are not selling, they are growing old on the hoof and they are costing a lot to feed. Why don't you sell? It's crazy to continue."

"No, I won't do it. It is all I have."

"Listen. You will soon have to hire men to work the farm. It will cost even more than now. Johann has passed on. His boys want to sell their sections. Louise tells me they are talking about going to California which would leave no one to work the farm. And George has no interest in the farm anymore. He is happy being a carpenter in town, even if he does help at harvest time. He has his boys, neither of whom have any interest in farming. Winnie will not have any interest in it as well, I am sure."

"I am not going to sell, Barbara. That is it. I will find a way."

Barbara got up from the table, went out to the porch, leaving her father at the table. Ten minutes later, she was back. "Daddy, here is what I propose to you. I am going to pay off the mortgage. Now. And you will owe me the money. You will pay me back when you sell the farm, which you will have to do sooner or later. You will soon be eighty years old. In the meantime, you can hire someone to help you, to do the manual work, with some of the money you will be saving by not having to pay the bank. While that is going on, prices for cattle may improve and we can find a buyer for the farm at a price that is right."

"My own daughter bailing me out. Circus money, for God's sake. Do you not think this is a blow to my dignity, Barbara? I can't accept this."

"Daddy, the farm is worth a lot of money. Much more than the damn mortgage. It is peanuts compared to the value of the farm. Just accept to do away with the need to scrounge. And Circus money. Yes, Daddy. Circus money, but it is the only way I can see to give you some peace of mind. I have the money. You have no idea what Mrs. Barnett gave me. But I can tell you it was enough to do what I am doing in Topeka....and pay off the damn mortgage. To avoid everyone in Wamego including Will and his father knowing what is going on, we will switch the mortgage to a bank in Topeka – you will say you found a lower rate of interest - then I will pay it off soon after. Nobody at Farmer's Bank of Wamego will have to know that. We'll tell Maggie but ask her to keep it to herself. Daddy, you don't have to have your reputation tarnished in any way. You can ease out of this and have a more worry-free life. Let me do it."

Within a year and a half, Josef had sold the farm for an acceptable price. Cattle prices had improved, helping the sale price of the farm. Joe Tauer retired to Wamego, paid Barbara back, and invested the rest of the money through his good friend and lawyer, Bill Sullivan. He moved in with Maggie and Will in the nice house they had on 5th Street up the hill from downtown, and Louise moved to Topeka to help Barbara in her shop and rooming house, and hopefully be successful in finding a husband. Nobody in Wamego or Westmoreland or Flush knew about the mortgage deal with Barbara. Joe Tauer could walk around Wamego with his dignity intact.

Chapter 13

TOM HAGEN

The short, wiry man, nattily dressed, with a stylish collar and silk cravat, rare for men in Topeka other than judges, lawyers and politicians, had entered the shop. "Can I help you, sir?"

"Yes. I am looking for a gift for someone. Perhaps you can help me. It is for a lady with good taste. Your shop has a reputation for fine ladies' things."

"This must surely be for your wife. Perhaps you can tell me about her tastes, what she would like – scarf, shawl, a pair of gloves, some fine material."

"No. Not for my wife. I am not married. It is for the wife of a dear friend who owns the house where I lodge. She is attentive to me and I am looking to thank her. Her husband is a lawyer here and recommended your shop. A scarf would perhaps be something we could consider."

"Well, always glad to hear of references given by people. Let's see what we can take a look at." Barbara turned and led the man over to a table arrayed with a number of silk and linen scarves spread across the table. "Here is a fine selection of silk scarves, direct from Paris. Some as well from Regent Street in London."

"Very good. I can see the lady would appreciate any one of these. I will let you pick one out for me. One lady for another."

"Very well. Most ladies appreciate silk. I would most like this one." Barbara took the scarf and spread it out over the table.

"Good. I defer to your taste, which I must say, is exquisite."

The man is a gentleman, thought Barbara as she enveloped the violet and burgundy scarf in fine paper and tied it with a ribbon. Kind. Thoughtful. But a bachelor. I wonder why. She looked at the man and gave him the package. "Thank you, mister…?

"Hagen. Thomas Hagen." The man turned and walked toward the door. "Thank you, ma'am."

"Oh, Mr. Hagen, just one thing before you leave. Who is the kind man that gave you the reference to my shop? I would like to thank him, if I know him."

"Oh, I think you know him. He is Ed Sloan. And he often dines at your house, I understand. That is what he tells me."

"Yes, Ed Sloan. I do see him often."

"Good day, Miss Tauer. And thank you once again."

A few evenings later, Barbara saw Ed Sloan sitting with two men she recognized as state senators, one of whom stayed at the house whenever the senate was in session. She went over to the table.

"Excuse me gentlemen. Senator Balderson, good to see you. And Mr. Sloan, good to see you as well. I hope you enjoy your meal. Senator Rivers, you are such a loyal customer. Glad to see you bring such acquaintances to our fine table."

"Miss Tauer, you are a gracious host. Your house here is the ultimate place of lodging in this town. Glad to be of service," responded the senator while nodding appreciatively to the lady.

Later, as the men rose and made their way to the door, Barbara caught up with Ed Sloan as he paused to gather his hat.

"Ed. I want to thank you for something. You suggested my shop to a gentleman the other day. A Mr. Thomas Hagen. That was nice."

"A pleasure, Barbara. Tom is a good friend. He has stayed with us since arriving in Topeka. We have a big house. Glad to have him. And glad to have put him on to you. My wife appreciated the scarf by the way. Top quality, as usual."

"Such a nice dresser, Mr. Hagen. What does he do? Where is he from? So rare to see such a fine dressed gentleman here who is not a judge or a senator or an attorney like you. Is he a lawyer?"

"Tom is from Illinois, but he's not a lawyer. He is the chief machinist for the Sante Fe. He gets his hands dirty, but you would never know it from the way he dresses, at least when he is out and about. And, he is a good Catholic like you."

"Very good, Ed. Just thought I would ask. Very nice man. Thanks once again for the reference."

Chief machinist for the railway, she thought. Probably has a lot of men working for him. Their shops on the other side of town are huge. Catholic from Illinois. Well. Maybe worth pursuing. Barbara had once again been thinking about finding a husband. Topeka is not such a big place. I will see him again. Perhaps at church. Someone the same age or a little older than me. Single. A gentleman. Not many like that in Topeka. I'm forty two, for God's sake.

Barbara changed her churchgoing the following Sunday. She went to the 9:30 Mass rather than her usual one at 11. There he is, she thought, seeing him across the aisle in a pew a few rows ahead of her.

"Mr. Hagen, so good to see you." She had made sure she had left her seat in time to be one of the first on the steps outside the church after Mass. Tom Hagen had come through the big open doors and had started down the steps.

"Well, Miss Tauer. I had no idea you were of the same faith. It is good to see you. I must say that Mrs. Sloan truly appreciated the scarf and the fine taste that led to its selection. I thank you once again."

"Mr. Hagen, I saw Ed Sloan the other evening and mentioned your visit to the shop. He took the liberty to tell me he was indeed a good friend of yours. He also said that you were from Illinois."

"What else did Ed Sloan tell you? Seems like you had a discussion about me, am I not wrong?"

"No, you are not wrong. I must admit. I am always curious about well-dressed, well-mannered gentlemen who are in this generally rough-edged town that was not so long ago on the edge of the frontier. I have travelled much in my life to date and have a curiosity about people."

"Well, perhaps we can talk about that sometime."

"Very well, Mr. Hagen. My house with its dining room is just on the other side of the park here. You can see it over there. I would be glad to have you for dinner some evening. My name is Barbara, by the way."

"And mine is Tom." The lady is being very forward. Seems to know her way around, he thought. Clear invitation to meet again. Maybe not such a bad idea. Not a bad looking woman.

Tom Hagen was fifty years old and a bachelor. He had been born in Queens County, Ireland and had come to America with his parents at the age of three. The family settled in Mattoon, Illinois, where his father operated a blacksmith shop, shoeing horses and making harnesses. Tom followed in his father's footsteps after spending but a few years in school. His father died suddenly at 45 when Tom was eighteen. He was an only child and had to look after his mother. There was no question of returning to Ireland, as there was nothing there to go back to. Times there in 1878 were no better than they were when they had left. He continued to work as a blacksmith, taking over his father's shop, but business was tough to come by. Many of his father's customers left to be served by other more experienced blacksmiths and the business floundered. While growing up, Tom had taken great interest in the workings of machines. He began to repair machines for manufacturers in Mattoon and became known more for that than for making buggy harnesses and shoeing horses. At 26, he closed the blacksmith shop and went to work as a machinist for the railroad. He learned the trade of building and repairing machines used in the maintenance of railway cars and locomotives as well as the machining of replacement parts for the company's rolling stock.

Within a few years, he had risen to the position of foreman. In those years, he also took the time to formally educate himself in technical matters, earning a certificate in industrial engineering from a technical institute in the town. He was devoted as well to his mother and stayed with her until her death from tuberculosis. At age 36, he was alone. He had never succeeded in developing a strong relationship with a woman. It just never seemed to work out, particularly given that he lived with his mother, who was often in ill health and dependent upon him. Mattoon was also not the greatest place to meet young women. Most were married by the time they were eighteen or nineteen. If you did not get one at that age, you probably would not get one. Time passed and Tom had remained single, spending much of his free time at the favorite Irish game of lawn bowling and at the increasingly popular game of golf. He became one of the best golfers of Mattoon and was a co-founder of

74

the city's country club. But after the death of his mother, Tom Hagen had no more obligations and wanted to move on with his life. He went to St. Louis where he found a job as a machinist with the Atchison Topeka and Santa Fe Railway, which had its eastern terminus there. St. Louis was the gateway to the West, a hustling, bustling center of activity, and rapidly becoming more cosmopolitan. It would never rival Chicago or New York, but it was alive and thriving. It was there that Tom Hagen developed a penchant for fine clothes and good living. He would often spend evenings on the riverboats tied to the docks on the Mississippi, dining and playing cards, sometimes going down river to Memphis and Jackson and back on weekends. He had a few lady friends in his years in St. Louis, but as in Mattoon, nothing serious developed. He came to think of himself as a bachelor for life. He was also Irish and Catholic. His mother had told him many times in the years before her death that his situation was no different from many of the men back in Ireland. Unmarried well into their thirties and looking after their mothers and fathers. "You will find your lass someday, Thomas. You are too good a man to stay alone forever." Many of the unattached women one came across in St. Louis could be said to be of dubious character, however. Tom saw firsthand how men could be drawn into the tawdry side of life at the gateway to the lands and riches of the West. He was careful. And, in 1910, the railway sent him to Topeka. Head machinist in the sprawling complex of the railway's center of operations.

In June of 1912, after close to a year of courtship, Thomas Hagen and Barbara Tauer were married. Barbara had told Tom she was too old to have children. Perhaps they could adopt, she had ventured. They would see. Tom was fine with that. Barbara was a lively, gregarious and informed woman who had travelled the world. He had surmised that there was perhaps no other woman in eastern Kansas that had a more cultured and informed view of the world. They became great friends as well as lovers, something neither one had experienced before. Tom also became a great friend to her father. "She has found a good man in that little Irishman," Josef Tauer told his friends in Wamego. "I just hope she doesn't boss him around too much."

As one of the wedding presents to his daughter and her new husband, Josef gave them the two framed paintings of his cousin Franz that Lizbeth had given him so many years before. Barbara promptly put them in the grand parlor of the rooming house. She told everyone who asked that the paintings were of her famous cavalry officer uncle who had gallantly led a charge at one of the key battles of the Austro-Prussian War and had been decorated for it. Josef never told her what his cousin had truly been through. "From where I am from. Austria. But I am a proud American now. We are all originally from somewhere else, are we not?" she would say to people when answering questions about the paintings.

Josef and Barbara and the rest of the family's connections with Austria had not been totally severed over time. They would re-emerge in early 1915. Josef received a letter one day from his brother Anton's grandson, Andreas Tauer, who he had of course never seen and did not even know existed. The wartime letter said that he had been conscripted into the Imperial army, had been captured on the Italian front in the war's early days. He had escaped, was living with an Italian family that spoke German and had an assumed name for the authorities. He had trained as a stone mason before the war and wanted to come to America. His father, who had passed away the previous year, had given him Josef's name and the name of the town of Wamego where he thought Josef was. He said he hoped the letter reached him. Would he receive him if he came? Josef responded immediately, writing back to the address given that he would be glad to receive his brother's grandson. Andreas Tauer arrived in Kansas in the summer of 1915. George took the young man into his home. He also brought him into his carpentry business. It was not untimely. There was a need for a stone mason for the construction of the new German-Bohemian church in Flush, not far from the former Tauer properties. One of the benefits of the arrival of the young Tauer was news of the family. Josef learned that his brother had died in 1889 of a fall from a horse and his sisters had both passed away a few years later. From what Andreas told him, he was once again thankful that he had brought the family to America. Things had not changed for ordinary people back home, despite what Barbara had told him about her travels in Europe. Andreas also spoke of the war that Austria was losing once again. His account of his time in the army reminded Josef of what Franz had told him fifty years before of the inherent inefficiencies of the Austrian military. "Thank God we are no longer there." Andreas's arrival also benefitted the Tauer women. Barbara, Maggie and Louise would spend time with him in the months after his arrival and learn of their ancestral home. He gladly obliged, telling of the family and of life in Bohemia. Andreas would soon start his own family and establish another branch of the Tauers in America.

Chapter 14

AMOS MULLER

Amos Muller was born in 1884 in Dauphin County, Pennsylvania. He was an only child and grew up on a farm. His father Aaron, who had emigrated with his parents from Bavaria as a young boy in 1854, had served in a Pennsylvania infantry regiment in the War Between the States. Amos' mother died when the boy was seven. His father took another wife and Amos left home at sixteen. He worked for a year for a blacksmith in a town not far from Cincinnati before finding work on a barge ferrying lumber and bulk goods up and down the Ohio River. At the age of twenty-three he quit the river trade and went to Kansas City. Not long afterward, he was hired as a clerk by the railway whose trains ran through the city. Gregarious and energetic, he was soon bored with the clerical job and applied to be a salesman for freight accounts. There were many German-owned businesses in Missouri and Kansas and elsewhere on the Plains where the railway operated and Amos could speak German. His father had always insisted on it. He got himself transferred to sales and rapidly became one of the top performing salesmen for the company. In the meantime, he acquired a reputation for having woman friends everywhere he went. He was a handsome man. It was that reputation that Tom Hagen, chief machinist for what was known as the Santa Fe, would eventually speak about with Barbara, and with Louise.

Muller had taken a room at Barbara's rooming house for the first time in the spring of 1915. He noticed the beautiful young woman who served at the breakfast table and cleaned the rooms. She noticed him as well.

He looks at me every morning. He is handsome and seems nice, looks to be a gentleman, thought Louise.

She is the most beautiful woman I have ever seen. I must have her, Amos told himself one morning. The next time he was in Topeka, he asked Louise to join him for a walk on the grounds of the legislature. She turned him down, saying it was improper to go somewhere with a customer of the rooming house. Muller was determined, however. He had come back to the rooming house because of her. When he saw her sitting on the porch of the house later that day, he went to her.

"Miss, I regret the awkwardness of my invitation to you this morning. I am sorry, but you are a very attractive lady, I must say, and I would very much like to get to know you. My intentions are totally honorable. You have nothing to fear. It is but an innocent invitation to take a stroll in the park across the street, in full view of the house and whoever you would want to observe our walk. What is your name, by the way? Mine is Amos. Amos Muller."

Louise looked at him. It was her first invitation in a long time. She hesitated. He was handsome, but Barbara wouldn't like it, she thought. I will accept anyway. "Alright. I will go with you tomorrow. It will not be necessary to have a chaperone observing from the house. I accept your invitation, but that is all. I really don't know you, and my name is Louise."

Chapter 15

Topeka, November 1915…

I will not be an old maid after all. Amos wants to marry me. Last evening I said yes. Barbara will be cross with me. Daddy will as well. I must tell them. I hardly know him, but I'm doing it.

Louise had been in Topeka for three years, working for Barbara in her shop as well as in the rooming house. It was a respite from the farm and the responsibility of looking after their father. Maggie had taken that over. Thank God. Daddy was living with her and Will, but it would not be for long, thought Louise. He's 85. Really looking old now. Sold the farm. George didn't want it, although he will have the money from the sale. Oldest son. Girls have to depend on their husbands.

I had young men propose to me. Luke from Nebraska. I was seventeen. He was so handsome. And gentle. Then, the men in the county, three of them over the years, three, but I could not accept. I would have if the men accepted to take Daddy as well. Not one of them wanted that. Basically the same every time. They had their own farm or business, like the handsome fellow from Rossville and they wanted me, without everything else that came with me.

Amos. How handsome. How dashing. So nice.

"You can't marry him, Louise. He is no good. I know." Tom, her sister's husband and a long time employee at the railway, was aghast. "He has a reputation for womanizing, Louise. You should not trust him. He rents a room here, he comes and goes."

"Of course, he comes and goes. That is his job. He is a salesman. Railway customers are all over, from St.Louis to Santa Fe and beyond."

"He is a womanizer. Everybody says it. You will be most unhappy, Louise."

"He will not be anymore, if he was. He says he loves me. I am the lady of his life, he says. Whatever he did before me, it is past."

"You will be sorry. I know you will."

"You and Barbara and Daddy are ganging up on me. I am 30 years old! This is my chance to have a husband, have children, have a life other than as a spinster cleaning rooms and fitting ladies in the back of a shop. My last chance and you are trying to ruin it!" Louise got up from the chair in the private parlor of the rooming house and went to her room.

"She is so naïve. That man will ruin her, Barbara" said Tom. "I told her what he was like, the reputation that he had. She won't listen to me."

"She has been the victim of my father's long life. She should have been free years ago, when she was in her early twenties. But Daddy needed her. I said I could pay for a maid. He said he could pay for one himself, but that was not the point. 'Daughters look after their aging parents. Period!' Said she would find a husband eventually. She was a beautiful woman, he said. Even at thirty or over she would find a husband. In the end, after she came here, he told me he was sorry. It was why he agreed to go live with Maggie and Will. Louise is not wrong, though. She has been here for three years and Amos is the first one to take real interest. You can't blame her. But this man Muller. I don't like it."

Barbara saw Amos one day on the street. The Sante Fe offices were one block over from Main Street where Barbara had her shop. He was talking with someone which allowed Barbara to catch up with him. As he finished the exchange, Barbara reached him, grabbed him by the arm and pulled him around to face her. "You sonofabitch, Amos Muller, I won't have you marrying my sister. I told you months ago to stay away from her. She is too good for you. I want you to call off the whole thing. Today! Now! You hear me, you no good philanderer!"

"Whoa! Now, now, Miss Barbara. Such language. Louise and I are going to marry. I love her. And you will never cuss at me again! Do you hear?!"

"I will cuss at you and call you what I want, Amos Muller. You are not to marry her. You will call it off. I will not have you fooling around all over this country and breaking her heart! She's too good for you."

"Miss Barbara, you will have to eat your words. Now, I must go. I have things to do. Goodbye."

"This is no good," said Josef as Barbara and Tom expressed their views of Amos Muller to him. They had driven to Wamego that Sunday afternoon. Barbara had told Louise they were going for a drive to Lawrence to see friends. "This Muller man. He hasn't come here to ask my permission."

"Louise has most likely discouraged him from doing it. She knows what you will think about this. And, I suspect he is not the type to go asking a father for the hand of a daughter. I am not surprised," said Tom.

"You know him, Tom. You say he is a womanizer."

"I know of him. I must say I do not know him personally. We have met twice, but only briefly. But he has that reputation. And he avoids me. He knows Barbara and I are against this. He doesn't stay at the house anymore when he is in Topeka. Has not for some time."

"I saw him on the street this week." said Barbara. "I really lit into him. I can't see us ever being civil now after what I called him. I ordered him to break it off. He refused."

"I can well imagine you getting into him, my dear," said Josef. He paused for a moment, looking out the window. "I won't allow it. I won't have my daughter marrying a man with that sort of reputation. You tell Louise to come and see me. You and Maggie will try to put some sense into her."

Maggie piped up. "Father, you kept her too long. That has a lot to do with it. There should be no surprise about all this. She is desperate to avoid living her life alone. She wants to have children. I will talk to her. Barbara and I will try, but it may not work."

"Has she spoken to you about it, Maggie?" asked Josef. "You two usually share everything."

"She has. I told her to wait, get to know the man better."

"She said she would. I guess she changed her mind."

Louise Tauer and Amos Muller were married in a small ceremony in Topeka in January, 1916. Maggie acted as bridesmaid. A co-worker of Amos acted as his best man. Barbara and Tom did not attend. Neither did the father of the bride. Josef Tauer died a week later, of a broken spirit, Maggie told a friend.

Louise was distraught at the death of her father. She took the blame upon herself. "I killed my Poppa," she told Maggie at the funeral in Flush.

"Louise, our father was 85 years old. He couldn't live forever." Louise felt enough guilt already. Maggie didn't want to lay on any more.

"But I killed him. He told me at Christmas he was so upset with me about Amos that he had trouble sleeping. You remember he was not eating at Christmas dinner. He said 'Amos, your man, is not even here, at Christmas, with the family'. I told him he was travelling. It's his job. Daddy was really upset. I killed him, Maggie."

"You didn't kill him, Louise. Don't take that on you. He was 85, for God's sake. Don't. Now Amos. Where is he? He's not here," asked Maggie.

"St. Louis. He had to go."

"His father-in-law dies a week after his marriage and he could not ask for some time off. Louise, I don't know about this. You and Amos. I hope he doesn't break your heart."

Louise and Amos had moved the day after the wedding into a small house that Amos had rented a few blocks away from the rooming house. Louise continued to help Barbara at her shop, despite Barbara's anger with her, but no longer worked at the rooming house. Amos travelled a lot, leaving Louise alone, sometimes for days on end. He had said he would quit the travelling job and seek something stable in Topeka after their wedding. As 1916 progressed, Louise saw little indication he would do that. Questioned on it, Amos said he had enquired, but had had no luck. Not many jobs available in Topeka. "You're not telling me the truth, Amos. Topeka is growing. There are many enterprises here. Barbara says business is expanding. Every business needs competent salespeople. I don't believe you."

"You will have to believe me, my dear. You are my wife and you should listen less to that nasty sister of yours. You must believe what your husband tells you."

"How are you two getting along?" Maggie asked Louise one day when visiting.

"All right. It's fine," replied Louise, not looking in Maggie's direction as she spoke.

"I mean with your marital obligation. In bed, my dear. How are you with that?"

Louise started to cry. "He is rough with me. It is not pleasant. I thought it would be more enjoyable. Momma told me when I think I was fifteen and before she died that life in bed with our father was wonderful and always had been. I was surprised she told me that. In any case, I thought it would be like that. I had looked forward to it. The great mystery before your wedding night. It's not enjoyable, Maggie."

Chapter 16

THE CHILD

In October of 1916, Louise learned she was pregnant. She was overjoyed. "I'm going to be a mother after all, Maggie. A Momma. I am so happy." As always, she confided in Maggie, something more easily done than with Barbara.

"Is Amos happy? Tell me. Are things getting better with you two?"

"He says he is happy. But I don't know, really. I've tried to be a good wife, but I just don't know with him. I would have thought he would hug me when I told him, but he didn't. He just stood there and said 'Good. Very well, my dear.' Then he sat down to the dinner I had prepared. I wanted to jump for joy, but he just sat there."

The birth of the little boy was difficult. Louise bled and the doctors had trouble stopping it. The baby was covered with a rash from head to toe.

The doctor who delivered the baby was with the attending nurse. "This is worrisome. I don't like what I see here. I've seen it before. Mother bleeding, baby with horrible rash all over. What I see here are the effects of syphilis. I think this young woman has been given what comes from that affliction. Poor woman. I'm sure she did not know. I know this family, her sister," the doctor said.

"My God. She could bleed to death," said the nurse. "Did you know or suspect anything?"

"Nothing," replied the doctor. "She never said anything about it. I didn't notice anything when she came to see me. But I think it comes from syphilis. Probably had it for awhile and did not even know it. The baby is not in good shape with the rash and the sores, but would be in worse condition if it had been transmitted to the mother during the primary stage. Her husband undoubtedly gave it to her. Knowing this young woman and her sister as I do, it would not be from anybody else. I will have to inform her family."

"How could this be, doctor?" asked Maggie. "Men who have syphilis are supposed to have sores on their penis, on their body. Our sister would have noticed it. How could that have been missed? I'm sure if she had seen something, she would have told you, told someone. I cannot imagine she would not talk to someone about it. You or even me. We have always shared things between us. She would have been in a panic. Syphilis. My God."

"Her noticing it? Not necessarily. The condition could have been in the latent stages, where nothing appears. It is in the early stages that the sores appear. He has probably had it for a long time. If that is the case, she would have noticed nothing amiss. Also, couples do not always see their spouses naked," said the doctor.

"That awful man," said Barbara as she turned and walked down the hall to the stairway.

"Madame, you can't come in here. This is the men's only lounge," said the waiter as Barbara charged through the door of the bar at the Kansan Hotel.

"Get away. I need to speak to somebody." Barbara saw Amos at the end of the bar with his back turned and went to him. "You gave her syphilis, you sonofabitch," hissed Barbara in his ear before he could turn around and see her, hoping she was not loud enough for the other patrons to hear what she was saying. "Louise could die. The baby is covered in sores. You are despicable, Amos Muller."

Amos turned, looked around the room, and saw that people were watching. Women were never in the bar. In a voice as low as it could be, he hissed back at Barbara. "Get away from me, woman. I do not have the clap. The doctor is wrong. Get out of here. I will take care of my wife."

"I bet you will. All the doctors at St. Francis Hospital cannot be wrong. I'm going back there now and make sure everything is done to save her. I suggest you stay away, Amos. I always thought you were a no-good philanderer. Now we know it to be true. Stay away. She didn't deserve you. I just hope we can save her and that little boy." Before Amos could respond, Barbara turned and left, leaving the other patrons staring and wondering what had transpired. An angry bull of a woman had just given a piece of her mind to someone.

"Wasn't that Mrs. Tauer, now Hagen or something, the owner of the rooming house that the politicians go to?" asked one of the men to another at the table.

"Yep. That's her. I wonder what the guy did to deserve that. She was some angry lady."

Louise cried out to Maggie and to Barbara. "Can anybody tell me what is wrong?" Nobody wanted to tell her. "Where is my husband? Where is Amos? Will somebody tell me?" Amos had come to the hospital, but Louise had been unconscious with doctors trying to stop the flow of blood. Barbara and Maggie were outside the room when Amos showed up. He tried to barge into the room. Barbara had foreseen his coming and had asked Tom and

Will to be there. They held Amos back. An orderly saw what was going on and came down the hall to help. "You can't go in there, Sir. Doctors are trying to save someone's life in there."

"That someone is my wife."

"I'm sorry, Sir. You can't go in."

Amos released himself from the grip of the men, turned and stomped down the hall and disappeared.

"Doctor, what is happening to me? I can't stop bleeding." Louise was weak, taking whatever of her energy she had just to speak. She had difficulty in sitting up.

"You have a condition that is difficult to correct, Mrs. Muller. Hemorrhaging related to childbirth. We are doing all we can to stop it." He was not going to tell her that her husband had syphilis and had transmitted it to her. Her sister had begged him not to tell her. If she was to die, she was not to know that her husband had essentially killed her. In his view, that is what it was. A form of murder. The man had known he had it. Would have to know.

"My baby. He has a rash all over his body," she said with a weak voice. "What is it?"

"We're not sure. An infection of some sort. Otherwise, he is healthy."

"I can't feed him. He cried the whole time he was with me. And the nurses won't bring him to me now. He has been with me just three times since he was born, but for never more than a few minutes. He screams. Doesn't stop. What does he have, Doctor? Please tell me."

"We don't know. We are doing all we can to determine that." He was not going to tell her. He had promised.

That evening, Louise was in and out of consciousness. Maggie was present and sitting next to the bed when Louise suddenly awoke, turned to her and blurted out "Syphilis. It's syphilis."

"What? Louise, what are you saying?" Maggie was aghast. How did she know?

"Syphilis. Nurses in the hall. I overheard them. They didn't know I was awake, but I heard them. I have syphilis, Maggie, and I am bleeding. My baby has it. He must. Amos gave it to me."

Maggie didn't know what to say, how to respond.

"Tell me the truth. Tell me. Is that what I have? Is that what has caused this?"

"No, Louise. It is childbirth. It happens. You will recover."

"You're lying to me, Maggie," said Louise with a frail, barely audible voice. "I heard them. I also heard one of them say 'her husband gave it to her.'"

"That is not true. You must rest. You will recover." Louise looked at her sister with half-closed eyes, tears slowly running down her cheeks, then slipped back into unconsciousness.

Maggie went to the hallway and found the nurse desk. She was angry. "My sister is down there in that room bleeding to death." The three nurses behind the desk were looking at Maggie. Nobody moved. "All it took to preserve her self-respect was for her not to know what she was dying of. Somebody amongst you spoke of her condition – that she had syphilis transmitted by her husband - in the hallway outside her room. She heard it. She is devastated. I am very angry." She looked at the nurse closest to her. "I don't know if it was you who spoke too loudly or whoever else it was, but my sister is destroyed because of what she heard."

"Oh, my God. We were sure she was asleep. She has been basically unconscious for two days. My God. I'm so sorry."

"I am just so angry," said Maggie, who then walked back to Louise's room.

Louise was semi-conscious. Somebody was next to the bed. She opened her eyes enough to see it was Maggie. She reached for her hand, took it, then drifted off again. Amos. Syphilis. I didn't know. I didn't notice. How could he? I should have known. They told me about him. I didn't believe it. I didn't want to believe it. So handsome. So gallant. I loved him. I thought he loved me. He said he did. Syphilis. What is it, really? Daddy, why didn't you ever tell me about those things? I'm dying. I know it. No. I can't. Robert. Little Robert. I told them his name.

Flashes of her life came. Maggie and me. The farm. Running through the fields. The butterflies, the fireflies we caught the summer nights. The prairie dogs we trapped, then lost. They always escaped. Maggie was so mad. She wanted to save them from the foxes. The times we dressed up. Momma and Daddy would laugh so hard. The costumes, the hats with the plumes. My first day at school. The boy who pulled on my pigtail and Maggie smacking him. None of the boys ever did that again. Maggie made sure. The first dance I went to. All the boys who wanted to dance with me. Poppa decided who got to. Maggie said I was the only girl there every boy wanted to dance with. She said I was the prettiest girl in the county, but that she was not jealous of it. Momma told me that. All those young men who wanted to marry me. I should have insisted to go. Lenny, the handsome boy from Alma was the sweetest one. He was so in love with me, but Daddy said no. When it is time, someone good for you will come along, he said. It is not the time for you. I need you. I was nineteen. I would already have a family. Amos. Where is your face? I can't see it. She opened her eyes. Maggie was there. "Look after him, Maggie." She then drifted off again.

Maggie looked at her sister who was wasting away, holding her hand.

Louise died two days later. The doctors could not stop the intermittent bleeding. She was conscious enough to hold her son for some precious moments a few hours before her death.

Chapter 17

The family had congregated at Barbara and Tom's. Louise had died that afternoon. The doctors couldn't save her. "She died as much of a broken heart as what that disease did to her," said Maggie. "My wonderful, innocent little sister. All she wanted was a family. He killed her."

Louise's little boy, seven days old, was at the hospital and in the care of the nuns and the nurses who kept him unclothed on satin pillows to alleviate the discomfort and pain of the sores that covered his body. The discussion turned to the child.

"Amos will not take the child. I won't allow it," said Barbara.

"You may not be able to prevent that, my dear," said Tom. "He is the father. It is his child."

"We can't have that happen. He is in no condition to take care of a baby, a sickly baby to boot. Acute eczema caused by the syphilis, according to the doctor. I can't believe he would do this to her."

"I will take the child," said Maggie. "I will raise him. I have been the closest to Louise all her life. You all know that. She would approve. Frances could be a big sister for him."

"How are you going to do that, Maggie? Deal with Amos?" asked Barbara.

"I'll find a way."

"Where is he, by the way? I want to hit him," said George. "I may be close to 60, but I'll smash him. Schlag him good."

"I haven't seen him since the run-in at the hospital." Barbara had thought about the child. The idea had been in her mind for a couple of days, since it became clear Louise would not make it. She needed to clear it with Tom. I will take the boy, she thought. I will be a mother, after all. She would talk about it with him later. "Let's make plans for the funeral. We'll do it at St. Joseph's in Flush. Everyone ok with that?"

That evening....

"Tom, I am going to take the boy. I have discovered that Amos has not made arrangements to pay the hospital or the doctor. If he does not do that in the next couple of days and I don't believe he will, because he doesn't have any money, I will take care of what's owed. He never has any money. Louise would always complain about it. He probably spends it all wherever he goes. I will pay the hospital and the doctor and the mortuary and whatever else and he will owe me the money and until he pays me, he will not get the boy. Before you object, which I can see you are the verge of doing, let me finish."

"Not objecting, Barbara. Surprised, yes, but I probably shouldn't be," responded Tom.

"Well, I spoke with Ernie Bentson about all this today. I saw him on the street. I explained to him what I wanted to do. He said he could draw up an agreement for it. He said that Kansas law provides for official adoption in time if the person owing has not paid the amount involved in a legal care of child agreement. Seven years. Ernie thinks that the fact he has syphilis, which I had to tell him, would be grounds for a judge to give me custody to begin with, but he said he can't be sure. Amos apparently has refused to be tested. An agreement with Amos may be the only way to do it. What do you think? I will have to force it on him. Do you want this? I sure hope you do, because that is what I want, Tom. Having a child."

"Maggie wants the boy as well. You are going to have a problem."

"She has one already. I don't."

Three days later, a Saturday afternoon, in Wamego, at Maggie and Will's. "I won't have it, Barbara. He has to come with me. I was closest to Louise. She would want it that way. She said 'look after him, Maggie.' And there is Frances, who could be a sister to him. With you, he will be an only child."

"No, Mag. You already have a child. This is my chance to be a mother like you, my only chance."

"At forty-seven, Barbara, and Tom at fifty-seven? Come on."

"Maggie, that's so mean. You shouldn't have said that."

"I wish I could say I'm sorry, but I am not. Who is going to look after him? You have two businesses."

"I'll do it. I will manage it all. In any case, you're too late, Mag. I've already paid for everything. I'm taking the boy, and that's final." Barbara got up, crossed the living room, walked out and slammed the door behind her.

Tom came out of the kitchen where he had been with Will. "Goodness, what happened? What's the ruckus all about?"

"The baby, Tom. He should be with me. Barbara is so stubborn."

"You both are."

"Well, we may be. What do you say about this? You're well over 50. Do you really want to have to look after a baby, through infancy, childhood, teenage years as an old man?"

"I'm staying out of it. This is Barbara's affair."

"Chicken. You can't stay out of it. You're part of it, whether you like it or not. You don't want to take her on," said Maggie.

"Maggie, I'm leaving. This is between you two. Strictly between you two. I have to leave. She's probably waiting for me in the car."

Will came out of the kitchen as Tom was leaving. "Will, she's done this to me," said Maggie as Tom closed the door. "Steam-rolled it. She knew I would want the baby, so she arranged everything in her name. Lawyer and all."

"You can be a favorite, doting aunt, Maggie. A second mother," said Will.

"Go to hell, Will Knecht! You are not being any help in this."

"Maggie, what I can see from all this is Barbara's only chance to be a mother. When it's all said and done, can you blame her?" Will looked at Mag, pacing back and forth. "I know you want that little boy, but this is a family affair. She has the means to support him, give him a good home in Topeka where there will be more opportunity for him. She will never have any children. We have a fine home here, but….Mag, don't be bitter about this. You will be able to dote on him all you want, and you will, I am sure of it."

96

"This is not over. Not over! In the meantime, that little baby is suffering. The nurses have to carry him around on silk cushions, for God's sake. I'm going to see Kewanee and her mother. Maybe they have something that we could put on the boy. I remember her telling me years ago about the special mixtures they had to cure things. Are you going to take me there or will I drive it myself?"

"I'll take you. You're so mad, you could drive the car into a tree."

"Let's go now."

"Mag, it's 5 o'clock already. We can do it tomorrow."

"No. Now."

Will Knecht's Model T reached the reservation at 6:30 and moved along slowly past the sign announcing the boundary of the Pottawatomie Territory. "I've never been here, Maggie. Where do I go? There are tracks going in all directions. There is no one here."

"Keep going. Take the track further along up to the right. Over the hill. I know this place and these people. I like them. I always have," said Maggie as the car trudged slowly over the rough terrain. "Did you know that Wamego is named after one of the chiefs of these people? Chief Wamego. Most of the people in town probably don't know that. This reservation covers now, I think, 11 square miles. At one time, these people had 100,000 acres in Iowa before they came here, much more before that when they were in Michigan, although the question of ownership of land was never part of their lives before the white men came along. In 1850, before Kansas became a state, the Pottawatomie reservation encompassed all of what is now Topeka and a huge area west of the city, halfway to Wamego. After statehood in 1856, they were relocated here with much more land than they have now, but a fraction of what they had before. Gradually all their land got reduced, taken from them."

"You used to talk to me about that. I never really listened. My folks were so anti-Indian. I never talked about these people, about you being friends with them. My Dad would have gotten really upset."

"Anyway, Will. Kewanee is a wonderful person. So is her mother, who is blind now. Keep going up the hill. Over the top, then you will see their houses."

"They're more huts than houses. Some are big tents," said Will as he maneuvered the car along the rough trail leading to the cluster of homes.

"Don't be so damn critical. These are fine people. Kewanee's father built the house at the end of that row of huts and tents on the left. Probably the nicest place on the reserve. I haven't been here in a while. When I was a little girl, their home was a hut." She looked off to the right and saw some people approaching. "Well, some people wondering who we are. An automobile on the reserve. Probably doesn't happen that often, although I can see a truck over there. Stop. I'll get out and tell them I've come to see Kewanee." She didn't have to say anything. Beshno, or Bald Eagle as he was known when they were kids, was one of the men and had recognized her. "I know them. Let them be," he said. "Maggie, good to see you. Welcome back, but so surprising at this time of day," he said as he reached the car. "Is there something wrong?"

"Well, there is and I wanted to talk to Kewanee. Is she here?"

"She should be. She works for a farmer near Onaga but she should be back. She and her husband live in Momma's house over there. I'll take you." The other men had dispersed. Will turned off the engine and the three walked to the house that looked recently painted, had a big porch, and a fenced yard on three sides full of wildflowers. Will looked behind the house and saw a field with rows of young corn, and what looked to be a smokehouse for curing meat with a watermelon patch next to it. On the side of the smokehouse was a rack of rabbits hanging, waiting for cleaning and skinning. Further back was a fenced-in area with three steers and a horse.

Kewanee opened the door, exclaimed her surprise, and threw her arms around Maggie. "My dear Maggie. What a surprise. What brings you here? Such a long time."

"Yes, a long time. I need to talk to you about something. This is Will, my husband."

"I know. Hello, Will. I remember you. Welcome. Come in, come in, both of you."

Maggie and Will entered the house. Kewanee's mother, Wawetseka, was seated on cushions on a bench that filled a corner of the large living area. "Mother, Maggie Tauer is here. You remember Maggie. She is with her husband. She wants to talk to me about something."

"I actually want to talk to you both," said Maggie. "Someone in my family…has a problem. I thought you may have a solution."

The old blind woman spoke up first. "What is the problem?"

"My sister Louise had a baby a little while ago. The little boy was born with a terrible rash over all of his body. There are sores as well. Louise died a few days ago, seven days after giving birth, of syphilis given to her by her husband. I am ashamed to say it, but you should know."

"Syphilis, you say," said the old blind woman.

"Yes. Do you know what that is?"

"Yes, I do. We have had men who had it and they were banished from the reservation. I know what it is and what it can do."

"I remember you had potions to cure things that came from herbs and roots. You told me about that when I was little. Would you have something that could treat the child? He suffers terribly. The nurses keep him on satin pillows to alleviate his discomfort. He cannot wear diapers, although he must. He screams when they are put on him."

"The rash covers his body, you say, and there are sores."

"Yes, like little boils."

There was a brief exchange between Wawetseka and Kewanee in their language. The woman then addressed Maggie. "I will have to touch the baby, feel his skin. I think I have something for this. Kewanee will be my eyes. We have to go to him, or he be brought to us. Can we see him, touch him some way?"

"He is at the hospital in Topeka. The nuns and nurses are looking after him. I don't think we will be able to bring him here. We will have to bring you and Kewanee to him."

"So be it. I can go any time. I will be glad to help you, Maggie. You were good to us. I think I may have something for this problem of yours. So sorry to hear your sister is no longer. I remember her. She was a beautiful child."

"Yes, she was. You are so kind, Ma'am. What about tomorrow? It is a Sunday. Kewanee?"

"No work tomorrow. If it is Ok with the hospital, we can go. Momma?"

"Yes, I can go. There is nothing keeping me here tomorrow."

"OK. I will make arrangements. I will come here tomorrow at 11 in any case. Whether we can see the baby or not. There is no telephone here, is there?"

"No, no telephone. There is little reason for us to call anyone from here. We live here, work here, talk directly in person to anyone we need to speak to."

"Alright, then."

"Very good, Maggie. I hope to be able to help you."

They got back to their house at 8:30 and Maggie went to the telephone. Barbara answered. "Hello, who is calling? Seems a bit late for a call on Saturday night."

Always bossy, thought Maggie. "Barbara, it's me, and you don't have to be so curt. I may have a solution for the baby's rash. From an Indian woman I have known for a long time. She says she may have a potion to clear up the rash and the sores. She has to see him. I am proposing we bring her to the hospital tomorrow so she can see, feel the little one's skin."

"An Indian potion. Come on, Maggie. Are you serious?"

"Barbara, let's not argue about the Indian stuff. You know how I feel about that. I know these people. They have developed treatments and cures for things that we have no idea about. Do you have any other solution? The boy is suffering. We have nothing to lose. I know you are hogging him, keeping him all to yourself. We will never agree on that. But, God damn it, let me try to find a cure for that little boy." Before Barbara could answer, she continued. "Now, Will and I and the Indian woman and her daughter, who has been my friend since I was eight years old, are coming tomorrow. We will be at the hospital at 2 o'clock. I expect you to be there and make sure the nuns allow us to see the baby. Do you hear me, damn it?!"

"Yes, I hear you, Maggie. I'll be there." Barbara hung up the phone. She turned to Tom, who was sitting nearby. "Maggie coming tomorrow with some Indians to see the little one. Some potion to cure the rash. Our doctors here are not good enough, I guess."

"Well, they may not be. They haven't found a solution yet. And, my dear stubborn lady, will you let your sister have some say in that little boy's welfare? She may have something. Indians have solved problems for themselves for thousands of years."

"Alright. In any case, I didn't have a chance to say no. They're going to the hospital tomorrow. I better be there."

The blind woman ran her fingers over the baby's skin – abdomen, thighs, forehead, cheeks, ears, feet. She said something to Kewanee in their native tongue. Kewanee replied in English. "The small sores are everywhere. They are all dry, Momma. The skin, more red than pink. Everywhere. You have felt the sores and the skin. This is what I see."

"Tell me more about what you can see. What is the color of his lips? Are they dry? Are they puffy? His testicles, are they more red than pink? Are there sores around his eyes, on his ears?"

Kewanee responded in their language.

The woman rose up. "It is what you call eczema, coming from the venereal disease of the father. That's what I thought based on what you told me last evening. I have something. I brought it with me. If you agree, we can rub it on his skin. Kewanee will do it. I think it will cure the rash, and the sores." She brought a small pouch made of animal skins out of her bag. "It is made of herbs and roots of plants that grow just about everywhere. We have used this to treat skin problems, infections you call them, over many lifetimes. My grandmother showed me how to make it. I had Kewanee get everything this morning and I ground and mixed it

102

with beef tallow before you came. It is like a cream. It does not smell very good, but it should work. Do you agree? It will not hurt him."

Maggie did not let Barbara say no, and did not look at her. "Yes, please go ahead." Barbara didn't say anything. Kewanee took the cream and applied it all over the whimpering, half asleep baby's body. To his torso, arms and legs, feet and hands, his cheeks, his forehead and head. "You will have to prevent him from putting his fingers in his mouth. It will require keeping his hands away from his face. Do not wash him today. Only tomorrow. Then re-apply the cream everywhere on his body. Just like I did. Do it for five days. You will see the rash go away."

"I'm going to do it," said Maggie. "I will stay here this week, with you and Tom, Barbara." She looked at her sister, who had said nothing since they had arrived in the room.

"It's not necessary, Maggie," said Barbara. "I will do it. You don't have to stay here. I'll do it."

"You believe in this now. You didn't last night," said Maggie.

"The baby is suffering. He's asleep but he frowns, whimpers, we all can see he is not well. I am going to do what's needed. I will come every day."

"Ok, Barbara. We have our differences about the boy, but I'm glad you go along with this." The two women looked at each other. Barbara nodded to her sister. "Let's bury this for the moment." She looked at the Indian woman. "I appreciate what you are doing. I'm sorry we have been this way." Maggie looked at Barbara, indicating with her eyes that maybe it was not a good idea to be talking about their differences in front of the others in the room. The nurse in attendance provided the vehicle for that.

"Mrs. Hagen, I will be here as well. I can apply the cream. You don't have to. I am his nurse. Please let me do it. It is my duty."

"Alright, I will be here every day, just the same," said Barbara. "I'll be with you when you do it."

"I propose to come back here next Saturday," said the elderly Indian woman. "Maggie, could you bring me? We will see how the little one is doing."

"Yes, of course," said Maggie.

As the Model T took them back to Wamego and the reserve, Wawetseka said to Maggie in her soft, measured voice. "My dear, what the little one has will be passed down two generations. His children, should he have any, will not have any symptoms of this. But the next generation, if there is one, will. Not every one of the descendants will have it, but certainly some. It is the nature of it. It could be severe in some cases. They will have it as children, and perhaps into adulthood."

"Damn that man who gave this to my sister, and his son and who knows how many others down the line."

"The boy does not have syphilis," replied the blind lady. "He has what comes with it. He will be immune from syphilis as will his descendants, but he will be vulnerable to other sicknesses, I'm afraid. It is the nature of it."

"What do I owe you, Ma'am?" said Maggie.

"We will see how it goes in the next few days. First things first. But I want nothing for myself. You don't owe me anything, Maggie. You were a wonderful friend to my children. That is enough."

The following Sunday..

Maggie and Will had picked up Kewanee and her mother for the trip to Topeka. As they left the reserve, Maggie told them she had heard from Barbara. "The rash is almost gone. My sister called me this morning. The cream seems to be working. The nurse told her yesterday that the boy was sleeping much better. We'll see this afternoon."

"That is good news. I knew it would work. It usually does. I am anxious to touch his skin and feel for myself," said the Indian woman, as she leaned back on the seat in the back of the Ford.

"He will be fine," she said after running her hands over the baby's body. "I don't think you will need this anymore," she said, touching the satin pillow. "You will be able to dress him soon. I suggest you continue the cream for five or six more days. There should be enough left."

"Yes, there is," said the nurse. "He is sleeping better now. And for longer hours. He's exhausted."

Chapter 18

She found him alone at the bar. It was the middle of the afternoon and only a few other people were there, sitting at tables.

"Ma'am, you can't be in here," said the bartender.

"You told me that a few days ago as well and I don't give a damn," replied Barbara. "I have to speak to this man and you are not going to stop me."

Amos turned towards the door and the looming figure of Barbara Tauer Hagen moving toward him. "Barbara, I've got nothing to say to you. Stop right there."

She continued to where he was sitting. He got up, moving to confront her. "Sit down, Amos. We need to talk. But I must say, not here," said Barbara as she quickly glanced around the room. All eyes were on them.

"I don't want to talk to you. I have nothing to say, and get the hell away from me," said Amos.

"We are going to talk, one way or the other. You can either come with me now to where we can talk, and I suggest we use the shop, or you are going to be served with a summons."

"A summons? What the hell are you talking about?"

"To appear before a judge and sign an agreement between us," replied Barbara.

"An agreement for what?"

"For the care of your son, Amos Muller, and for the terms of your repayment of all I paid out for Louise's care, if and when you can do that. You will not be taking that little boy until you do."

"Ma'am, you have to leave." The bartender had caught up with Barbara. "Take your argument with the gentleman elsewhere. No women allowed in here, period."

"He's no gentleman, and I'm not leaving unless he comes with me."

"Well, you will have to. I'm calling the police."

"Beat it, Barbara. I'm not going anywhere with you," said Amos.

"Alright, then. The summons it will be. This will all be in the form of a court order by a judge. Imposed on you. Goodbye. And to hell with your rule, Mr. Bartender." Barbara glared at both men, turned and walked out.

"Ernie, I need you to serve the deposition and get the judge to rule on this. No cooperation from Amos. Can we get this expedited?"

"I think so. Circumstance of the boy in hospital will get it handled. Pretty sure." Ernie Bentson called Barbara the following day. "Saw Judge Shelton this morning. Showed him the deposition. He wants to call a meeting in his chambers. He is ordering a summons to be sent to Muller."

"Mr. Muller, since you can't take care of the costs of care of the boy and of his late mother, and you are not in a position to care for the baby going forward, as I understand it, I suggest you accept what Mrs. Hagen is proposing to you, which by the way, conforms to Kansas law regarding matters of this nature. You have read the deposition, I gather. Will you agree to this on your own, or will the state have to impose a decision in its place?" The judge was not wasting time. He looked at Amos and then at the lawyer Amos had brought with him. "Counsel, do you have anything to say regarding this? Have you read the deposition?"

"Yes, I have. I have advised my client to not sign the document, certainly not now, based on what he has told me about the substance of all this." Amos then spoke up before his lawyer could continue or the judge could say anything more. "This all stinks to high heaven. I object."

"You can object all you want, Mr. Muller, but I am on the verge of ruling on this. My decision could very well place restrictions on you, including contacts with your son over time, that are far more onerous than what Mrs. Hagen here has proposed to you. As a judge, I have the authority to do so. I suggest you sign the agreement. In seven years, or upon which time you manage to pay off what is owed Mrs. Hagen and have complied with the restrictions in the agreement and demonstrate you can provide a healthy family atmosphere for your son, you will be able to gain custody. Otherwise, you may never see him again, if it's left up to me. The agreement here gives you visiting rights, by the way. I could take that right away, given other aspects of this matter. Do you hear me?" Amos' lawyer responded, "I wish to speak to my client. Will you excuse us for a moment?"

"Certainly. There is a small conference room through that door." Five minutes later, Amos and the lawyer emerged. The lawyer appeared flustered and said nothing.

"Well, Mr. Muller?" asked the judge.

"I strongly object. I won't sign," replied Amos. "You can't make me do this. The boy is my son."

"Alright, Mr. Muller. I will go a bit further here. I understand you have an affliction and that you transmitted that affliction to your wife, which caused her death, according to the doctors at St. Francis Hospital. You surely knew what you had and knowingly transmitted the disease to your wife, which is known to ultimately cause death. You could be accused of murder, Mr. Muller. The district attorney could be very interested in hearing about it. I will not tell him, as I am a judge and must recuse myself from any matter of the sort, given this meeting, but somebody else could. I think you had better sign the agreement with Mrs. Hagen. Counsel, I would suggest that this could be the most prudent course for your client."

"Hold on here. You are being very forceful," replied the lawyer. "Almost beyond your authority, Your Honor. This is not a courtroom."

"You know damn well I can do this, counsel. So shut up if you have nothing more to say about the matter at hand. What will it be, gentlemen?"

The lawyer looked at his client and nodded, then looked back at the judge. Albert Shelton had been a judge for over thirty years and it was generally viewed by the legal community in Topeka to be unwise to cross him. The lawyer clearly did not want to be seen to be doing that. "Mr. Muller will sign the agreement."

"I'm sorry, Maggie, but I now have legal custody of the baby. A legal agreement with Amos, sanctioned by a judge. I went forward with it. I'm sorry it had to be this way."

"It didn't have to be. You proceeded with this on your own. It should have been discussed with the family."

"It was. The family is just you and George and I now. You had your say. I just didn't accept it." Barbara looked at her sister. She did not want the conflict to drag on, affect their lives any more than it had. "Maggie, you will be his loving aunt. You will love him and I'm sure he will love you. You will be able to see him anytime. You will be able to bring him to Wamego any time, spend time with you and Frances and Will. I will see to that.... Let's drop this. The agreement with Amos is done. The boy will be protected as much as can be done under the law."

"How are you so sure of that? What does the agreement say? He IS the boy's father."

"The agreement says he can only take the boy if he pays me the full amount of what I paid the hospital, the doctors, the mortuary and the church. Close to eight hundred dollars, which he does not have any way of paying, AND can demonstrate to a court that he is in a family situation where he can provide a decent home for the boy. He has seven years to do that, and at the end of that if he has not demonstrated that and has not obtained a release from the agreement, he cannot reclaim the boy. Tom and I will become his legal parents, although we will have to formally adopt him. All this according to Kansas law. Now, he could possibly find the money and somehow find a woman to provide an acceptable home environment, but you and I both know that is unlikely to happen. The man has syphilis. He will deteriorate. We know what happens to people who have it. I don't think he will ever be able to comply, but that is the limit of what the law provides to protect the boy."

"It's not foolproof. He could do it, come back, pay you back, convince a judge he is on the right track, and take the boy."

"He won't, Maggie. He's sick and he's broke. He always was. Tom says he will probably lose his job. If the railroad finds out about all this, he will be done. I have a mind to spread the word in Topeka. It can be done, but our lawyer says to stay away from that. Doesn't think it will be necessary. The only thing I fear is Amos kidnapping the boy. That's what I really fear. He has visiting rights, which I had to agree to, according to the law. We will have to be very careful." Barbara looked at her sister. "Maggie, can we bury the hatchet? I don't want this poisoning our relationship forever. I understand your disappointment. You and Louise were close, closer than I ever was to her. Please accept this. May we make the best of it?"

"Alright." Maggie saw that with the agreement sanctioned by the court, Barbara had won. She was the legal guardian and she might as well accept it, make the best of it. "You have a child now. Let's make sure he grows up to do justice to Louise. I will be his loving aunt, as you say, and you may even tire of that. I intend to be very present in his life. And I believe George intends to do the same, along with his kids. This is a Tauer affair. In the meantime, we must make sure we keep him out of the hands of that no-good father. Now, what will we call him?"

"Bobby. Louise apparently made the request to the hospital that his name be Robert. Before she went into the coma, I gather, and without us knowing it. Nobody from the hospital told us until I went for his birth certificate as part of the paperwork for the agreement. He apparently wanted the name to be Aaron, his father's name, but the hospital had already recorded the name of Robert on the certificate and nobody got around to changing it. Amos could have insisted on the name of Aaron for the agreement, but he didn't. Goes to show you just how much he cares for the boy. So, his name is Robert and I am sure it will be Bobby for short. Officially Robert Muller until I can adopt him. For everybody we know, he will be Robert Hagen."

Chapter 19

Wamego, July 1917

What is this.... thought Maggie as she saw the group turning the corner and walking down the center of Main Street. It had been a month since Louise's death, the funeral and the aftermath with the child. She was looking to get back to normal, but there was something going on. People with signs. She could make out a few. Go Home Germans! Throw the Krauts Out! A sheet held up with poles had a sketch of a crude Uncle Sam with his foot pressed to the throat of a soldier with a spiked helmet lying on the ground. There were more people behind the ones with the signs. It has come to this, she thought as she looked around. There were many people of German descent in Wamego, some who had arrived but a few years before. They generally got along well with everyone. Despite that, she could see some people down the block cheering as the parade made its way up the street. She looked across to the post office and the general store. There were people she knew - Lucy Umscheid, lady Schrieber, and old Henry Schultz looking at the parade, then turning almost in unison and going back into the general store. Other people stopped and watched. She turned around and saw the sheriff and his deputy entering the street from further up and moving to confront the demonstrators. The sheriff, with hand raised, reached the front row. She could hear him say to everyone to stop, to not go any further. The demonstrators surrounded the sheriff and his deputy. An argument ensued. The sheriff raised his pistol and fired a shot in the air. Everyone froze. Anyone who was in a store when the procession began was now outside and watching. There was some jostling; the sheriff fired another shot in the air. "Disperse! Damn it, disperse!" "We won't have this in Wamego!" At that moment, two other men who Maggie recognized as having been deputized by the sheriff in the past came running down the street with billy clubs in hand. The leader of the demonstrators, who Maggie did not recognize, tried to grab the pistol away from the sheriff, yelling at the same time, "Kraut lover! You damn Kraut lover!", then something about "we will march anyway." The situation was getting out of hand. As the jostling continued, Maggie saw the mayor emerge from the building where he had an office. He had a rifle and fired a shot in the air. Everyone froze once again. He walked to where the demonstrators were, pointed the rifle at the leader and said for everyone to hear, "You get the hell out of here and don't come back, whoever you are. And everybody else with him, the same! Not here in Wamego. The war is over there, not here! You hear me? Now!" Turning to the crowds that had lined the streets, he said "Whoever cheered for this should be ashamed. We have many fine German people here. Fine people, and you know it. They have nothing to do with what the Kaiser is doing over there. That is why most of them are here – to escape what they were living back home. They and we are all Americans now. So go about your business. This incident is over. Now, will you people here in the street leave or do we start arresting you?"

"For what, mayor? Demonstrating peacefully?" yelled a man in the back of the crowd.

"For inciting violence and disturbing the peace. Now do we start doing that or do you leave and get the hell out of town?" The demonstrators began to disperse. Maggie could see that some of them were residents of Wamego. She recognized a few of them. There would be problems in town because of it. She turned and walked toward their street and saw Will walking quickly from where the bank was. He waved to Maggie and caught up with her. "This almost got out of hand, Will. Thank God for the mayor and the sheriff and his deputies. Did you see who was involved?"

"Someone came into the bank and said there was a riot going on. We all ran out. I was far away but I thought I recognized the leader, the guy the sheriff was confronting when the mayor spoke. From Manhattan. A rabble-rouser. He came in for a loan a few months back. We turned him down. He was nasty about it. Said we would pay for it. That we were humiliating him. I remember him saying something about damn Germans being officers of the bank. It was just after the president declared war. I am not surprised it was him."

Will and Maggie learned later that the previous week had seen anti-German demonstrations in Manhattan, in Alma down the road and in Marysville to the north. Demonstrators in Alma had thrown eggs at German-owned businesses, rocks through the windows of others. There was an effigy of the Kaiser paraded down main street along with signs of 'Go home Germans'. In Alma and Manhattan, people with German names had been advised to stay home and many of them did. Wamego had been spared property damage but bad feelings would linger. "Many, many immigrants here. This may continue. This damn war," said the manager of the post office to Maggie.

The war would soon come close to home.

George's eldest son, Albert, 22 years old, opened the envelope. The letter was from the Selective Service office in Topeka. He was being drafted. He was to report to Fort Leavenworth for induction into the army on September 1.

"I will be fighting Germans. We are German, even if we are of the Bohemian branch. We're still German," he said to his father who had arrived home at the same time and had seen the dismay on Albert's face. "I suspected this would come. When the law passed a few weeks ago, I knew it. You and Leo would be prime candidates. I knew it."

"I don't want to kill anybody, Dad. This is not our war. It's the war of the French and the English."

"It is America's war now, Albert. And you and your brother are Americans, as are all of us Tauers now. You have no choice but to go. Let's pray to God you make it through it all and you don't have to kill anybody, German or otherwise." At that moment, Andreas, George's cousin who had fled the war, and had been living with them since arriving the year before, walked in. He saw Albert with the paper in his hand and George with his hands on Albert's shoulders. They looked at Andreas, who instinctively suspected what was happening. He said in German "You are being called up. I know it. The look on your face, the paper. Just like when it happened to me."

"Yes, I am being called up. To kill Germans and maybe Austrians as well, our blood brothers," responded Albert in German. Andreas was not fluent in English yet. When they could speak German, they did.

"At least you will be on the good side of this war", said Andreas, who had officially changed his name to Andrew a few weeks after arriving in the United States. "They deserve to be beaten. Germany has become a mean society. Arrogant, cruel to others. I saw it. At least you won't be fighting Austrians or Bohemians."

The men in the room had been living the effects of the war already. There had been the demonstrations directed against German immigrants, many of whom did not yet speak English. George's children had been born in America and they had no

German accents, but they had German names and some people let them know it.

This is terrible, thought George. My boys. Having to fight our own people. Will they take Leo as well?

A week later, Albert's brother Leo, a year younger than he, received a similar letter.

"Our boys. Pray be to God they live through this," George said to Mary. "Hopefully, the war will be over before they get to any battlefields."

"George. We can't lose them. I don't know what I would do," said Mary.

"I don't know either. Winifred will be upset. Both her brothers going off to war."

Winifred Tauer, 10 years old, was excited about having a little cousin. She would also, like Frances, be a big sister to Bobby. But her brothers, her dear big brothers who she adored and who had always looked after her, were going off to war. "Why, Daddy?" she asked her father. "What have the Germans done to us?"

"They are going to serve the country, my dear. Your brothers will come back, Winnie. I am sure of it… What have the Germans done to us? It is not the people, it is the country. Germans are kind people, just like us. But the country under its leader has become a danger to the world. Austria, where we come from, fought a war with Germany. We were attacked. I was a boy. I remember it. Your grandpa's cousin fought in that war. He was destroyed by it. You know those paintings in Barbara's parlor? They are of him, Uncle Franz, before and after that war. Germany is a danger to the whole world, including America. America has to protect itself. That is why." The discussion was difficult for George, who had married late in life and thought he would never want children after seeing his mother lose so many babies and be so distraught about it. But he was devoted to his offspring. With the boys leaving, not certain to return, he was determined to get closer to his daughter. He could see the tears in her eyes. "In the meantime, you will have me all to yourself, Momma as well. And you can help look after little Bobby."

"Yes, I will do that. He's so tiny and lovable. I held him for a long time when we were there. I loved Aunt Louise. She was so sweet, so kind, and so beautiful. She would come here and tell me stories, rock me to sleep. I miss her."

"Yes, she was a wonderful person. But as Bobby grows older, you have to promise me you will never tell him about his real mother. Louise will be his aunt Louise for him, who got sick and passed away. He must not know she is his real mother. His mother now is Barbara. And his father is Tom."

"But he will find out, Daddy."

"Not if no one tells him. You are to keep the secret. Can you promise me that?"

"Yes….I do. I promise. I understand."

Topeka Herald-Journal, September 15, 1918, General Notices

Declared insane. The State of Kansas has declared Amos G. Muller of Topeka, current address unknown, officially insane. Mr. Muller has been committed to the Topeka State Hospital for the Mentally Ill.

"Barbara, now we know why we have had no sign of Amos. Come and see this." Tom showed his wife the article.

"Officially insane. Good Lord."

"What did the doctor say? Advanced syphilis? That's what happens. We know now why he's been out of sight."

"He hasn't paid the rent on his house. The owner saw me the other day and wanted to know if we knew where he was," said Barbara. "I said I had no idea. But he's still in Topeka, even if it's at the hospital. We will have to be vigilant."

"People escape that place. There are no fences over there," said Tom.

Barbara looked once more at the paper on the table. "I don't believe for a moment he will not try to come and try to take the boy. Sane or insane. And I'm worried about this place here. It's open. People come and go at all hours. Amos could walk in anytime, come into the back here, overcome Maria or me and take him. I've been thinking of buying another place, just for us. Keep this, have Al and Kate look after it. Maria could come with us and look after Bobby."

"Or you could sell the shop and better spend your time here and with Bobby."

"You're right, I think. I can't continue with both of these businesses. In any case, I'm tired of hats and corsets and ladies that can't make up their minds. And we need a safer environment for Bobby. I am going to look for another house."

A month later, a big house one block away on Harrison became available for anyone who wanted to buy it. The owner and his wife had succumbed a few weeks before to the influenza epidemic that was ravaging the country – the great Spanish Flu of 1918. Barbara had been fearful of it and had kept Bobby at home for weeks, not even going out for walks. She had the city inspect the house she wanted to buy. It was sprayed for bugs, quarantined for two weeks, then inspected again. It was declared livable. By that time, the influenza had ceased to spread in Kansas. Barbara, Tom and the little boy moved into the house. Uncle George built a covered screened porch at the back for the boy to play in. A swing was hung from a branch of the big elm tree behind the house, even though the boy would not be able to swing on it for awhile. It would, in time, be a favorite for him all through his childhood.

As George helped with the renovations, he received news from his sons. They were in France. "What news do you have?" asked Barbara.

"They are in France, but I don't know where. Can't even tell you if they are in the front lines. Lot of stuff blacked out. Censors. Albert wrote it. Leo is in the same unit. Worried to death, dear sister. The news is all about setbacks. Big losses in battles. I just don't know. We worry about it all the time."

Three weeks later, Will had come in the door after work. He looked at Maggie, who was seated in the parlor. Something had happened. "Mary got a letter from Albert today," she said. "Leo has been wounded. They had to amputate his leg below the knee. He lost a lot of blood. He's in hospital in France. At a place called Chateau Thierry. I'm going to church with Mary tonight to say a prayer. The Great War has not spared the Tauer family, I'm afraid."

"He's been lucky, if he can make it through it," said Will. "Six boys from Wamego dead so far, according to the newspaper. Sixth one announced today. Len Brooken's boy. May Albert be spared."

A few weeks later, the armistice was announced. The slaughter had ended. In early December, George and Mary received a letter from Albert saying they would be home in January. They had done their service to country. Leo would be with him.

Chapter 20

Salina, Kansas, December 1918

"Momma, I really like it here. I have so many friends. It is so much more fun than back home." Frances Knecht, nine years old, had been at the convent school since the beginning of the school year. Maggie and Will had visited her every other Sunday since then, religiously making the trek from Wamego. They had been worried that their daughter would not adjust well at the start. Frances' best friend had been accepted the previous year and she had begged her parents to let her go there as well. They relented, but not without misgivings. It had been a good move, in the end, with the little girl clearly happy with the school and her surroundings. They could certainly afford it. Will had a comfortable salary as the assistant cashier at the bank, recognized one of the key figures in the town. The Christmas holidays were two weeks away and they had much to celebrate. Albert and Leo were on the way home from the war. The success of Maggie's theatre troupe. Will's status at the bank. There was Frances' happiness with her school, along with the good health of Bobby, her endearing little nephew.

This is good for Frances. She will receive proper schooling, and grooming as a young lady as well, thought Maggie as she looked at her daughter, seated in the parlor of the convent residence. Other parents were with their daughters, with some taking them to Sunday dinner at the town's famous restaurant, renowned throughout Kansas for its fried chicken, mashed potatoes and creamed corn.

Maggie and Will and Frances would be having some of that as well later that afternoon.

"How are you doing with your subjects, my dear?" asked Maggie.

"I love the subjects, Momma, especially literature and writing, but not mathematics so much. We have a lot of catechism. And next year, we will have Latin. I'm not sure about that."

"Well, it is a convent school. I almost went to one when I was younger, the one in Leavenworth. I wish I had. In a way, we are doing for you what I should have done for myself. But this is for you. We just want you to be happy."

"I am, Momma, but I am so lonesome for Bobby. He's like a little brother."

If you only knew how close that was, my dear, thought Maggie. "Well, you will see him at Christmas. A lot. Aunt Barbara says he will spend most of the holiday time with us. Now, let's go have one of those chicken dinners."

Later, on the trip home, "Things are going well now, Maggie. Time I get a newer car. Going to Salina and to Topeka every weekend requires something more robust. This one is getting rickety."

"What do you have in mind?" asked Maggie.

"Joe Daylor showed me a Chevrolet the other day. Gave me a price. I think I'm going to do it. We'd have the second nicest car in Wamego, right after Ralph's Cadillac. I couldn't have one of those, although we could afford it."

"No, you couldn't. It would cause a real problem with him and you don't need that. And we can use the difference between their costs to spruce up the house. Some new parlor furniture. And you now being the head of the Chamber of Commerce means we will have to entertain more."

"That we will. Meiner's has some new items. Nice stuff from Philadelphia, according to Gus. We should go see him this week."

"Ok. With Lucy doing the housework, I have the time. We can do it Tuesday or Thursday. Monday I have bridge, of course and you know Wednesday and Friday afternoons and early evenings are for rehearsals."

"I'm glad we have her. I never saw you being a housewife forever."

"You're right. Momma never wanted me to do the house stuff. I didn't do it very well." After a long bout of silence, traveling through the procession of small towns on the way home, Maggie spoke up. "The new Chamber of Commerce thing for you, Will? How much does it pay? You never told me."

"No pay. Not for me anyway or anybody on the board. I think that's the reason Ralph turned it down, then the board asked me if I wanted to do it. Only the staff gets paid, but there are worthy advantages, such as being aware of everything that happens in town, although being at the bank tells me just about everything to begin with."

"You get along pretty well with Burroughs, don't you?"

"He's not an easy boss, like Davidson was. He keeps many things to himself. Has meetings with people where he wants to be alone on the bank side. A bit strange. Pleasant enough, though. The accounts he looks after seem to be in order, but he's not as open as Fred was. Sometimes I feel I am not aware of everything that I should be."

Will and Maggie continued on to Wamego and home. As they drove down Main Street, Maggie looked at the quaint old stone building where her theatre group put on their productions. It had been a Baptist church and was shuttered for years after the congregation petered out. A few years before it had been taken over by the town for citizen use and became a theatre for plays and recitals. She was amazed at how elegant it was. "The town did well. George and Johann's boys did a great job on it. We have a beautiful little theatre now. All we need is our own Sarah Bernhardt to get people coming from elsewhere."

"You could be it, Maggie," responded Will as they approached home. "The play this fall was sold out every evening, and people I've talked to say the success was due to you. You were great."

"Lenora was supposed to play that character, that mean, vindictive woman," said Maggie. "I never thought I could do it. Not my nature. I prefer comedy. Making people laugh. But it worked out OK. I actually had fun being somebody I'm not."

"Not like you, to be sure. Bubbly, funny Maggie playing a nasty. Maybe this is the beginning of fame for you."

"From a little theatre troupe in Wamego, Kansas. Not likely, Will, but a nice thought. Thank you, my dear," she said as they turned into the lane. "Let's get to bed. These are long trips. Maybe I'll dream of being the Sarah Bernhardt of Kansas."

A year later.....

Will Knecht had just gone to bed. There was a knock on the door. He was alone as Maggie had gone to Denver two days before for a weekend of shopping with another lady from town. She would also be meeting a theatre booking agent who had heard about the plays of Wamego and wanted to meet her.

He went down the stairs and opened the door. It was the deputy sheriff. "Will, Ralph Burroughs shot himself a couple hours ago. You need to know it. You are now the key person at the bank."

"What?... Ralph Burroughs committing suicide? My God. Suicide. Are you sure?"

"Yes I am sure, unfortunately. Not pretty. I was the one who responded to the missus' call. Took a gun to his head. Gruesome. I hope I don't ever have to see that again. You don't know what could be behind it, do you?"

"No. I don't." But as Will said it, he knew what it was about. It had to be. The secret stuff, keeping the main account books in his office, in his safe, not sharing information on major loans and repayments. The President had apparently received a visit from the bank inspector the week before and had barged into the bank afterwards, going directly to Burroughs' office. Neither of them wanted to tell him what was up.

"Well, you may want to get to the bank early in the morning. There will be a lot of chatter and speculation about this. Burroughs was not particularly liked, if you permit me to say so, and of course, a lot of people in this town have their money there."

"Yeah, I guess he wasn't. Fred Davidson was a different type. Gregarious, personable. Ralph was not. But suicide. Yes...I will have to be there early."

After the man had left, Will called Maggie's hotel in Denver. "Maggie, Ralph Burroughs committed suicide tonight."

"What? Suicide?"

"Yes. Strange. I suggest you come home tomorrow. Things may be a bit dicey at the bank and we should be together at the funeral."

"My Lord. His poor wife...his children. I can't imagine what they are going through. I'll take the train tomorrow. We've done all we can here anyway. My God. What a tragedy."

The next morning, Will brought the employees of the bank together before they opened for the day. "As you probably know, Ralph is no more. I was informed last evening that he had died. It's a terrible thing. Many of you know his wife and his family. They will be going through a rough time. As for here, we will be opening as usual. Business must go on."

"He shot himself. That's what they're saying, Will," said one of the tellers. "Is it true?"

"I'm afraid it is. You might as well know. It's probably all over town this morning. Very unfortunate. I don't know what else to say. In any case, I will be assuming Ralph's duties about approvals, the signing of drafts, and the like. The President will be here to go over the status of official documents Ralph handled. People may be concerned about their deposits. We must allay their fears. The deposits are insured. The cashier of the bank may have taken his life, but the bank must be seen to be on solid footing, which it is. So, it is business as usual. You may direct customers to me if they wish to speak to someone in charge."

The morning after the funeral, Will was at his desk before the bank was to open. He got there early, going over records he had taken from Burroughs' office, from the safe he had managed to get into the day before, trying to find what may have caused his boss to shoot himself. The President, Carroll, was not telling him anything. Things are not adding up, he thought, as he finished going through one of the ledgers. There was a commotion on the floor. He pushed everything aside and went out to see what was happening. Three men he did not recognize were just inside the front door, with one of them arguing with one of the tellers who had opened it for them. "Gentlemen, I told you we are not open yet."

"I heard you the first time, but you are closed now," replied the man.

"Sir, I have no idea what you are talking about. We are not open yet and you will have to leave. You can come back at 10."

"You don't understand. I am sorry, but I explain. We are here to close the bank until further notice. I am deputy chief inspector of banks for the State. Please direct me to the new cashier's office, if there is one, or to the President. He should know we were coming. We are sorry to hear of the passing of the cashier. But there must be someone else in charge now and we must have the President here, in any case."

Will was stunned. Closing the bank. It's come to this. Burroughs. He crossed the floor and addressed the man who had spoken, interrupting the teller before he could continue. "Sir, there is no new cashier. I am the assistant cashier and responsible for operations for the time being. Please come to my office. Mr. Carroll, the President, does not have an office here, although I will get him here for you. His law office is across the street. Can we discuss this in my office?" said Will as he looked around. All the employees were looking at the gathering. The suicide of their boss, now something about closing the bank. Nobody moving. Worried looks. "Continue your work, everyone," said Will. "Gentlemen, please come to my office."

When they got to Will's office, the inspector closed the door and addressed Will. "We will be taking over your office. The cashier's office will be sealed. We are taking over operations of the bank. We have much to look into."

Will looked at the three men who were taking in everything in the office, very much acting like they were in charge. "I am not aware of any irregularities which could cause this. Surely there must be an error. The inspection was carried out weeks ago and as far as I know, nothing was deemed amiss."

"There is no error, and you have been perhaps misinformed. You could also be arrested. There were irregularities. Amounts, large amounts unaccounted for, as it turned out. We informed the President and Mr. Burroughs about these in correspondence. The response and explanations from the bank have been deemed inadequate. Significant sums, totaling over twenty thousand dollars, have not been accounted for. Surely you must know all this as assistant cashier. I suggest this could be at least part of the reason Mr. Burroughs took his own life."

"I'm sorry. I am not aware of any of that. I have not been privy to your dealings with Mr. Burroughs or the president. I am not aware of any missing funds." But Will knew it. The secrecy. Ralph and Carroll behind closed doors. Burroughs had insisted on responding to the inspection and said afterwards that everything was all right. Everything in secrecy. Twenty thousand dollars. Where did it go? That little agreement I had with him. Should never have done it.

"Mr. Knecht, I advise you to be careful about all this. Your saying you are not aware of missing funds or of any irregularities in the accounts, given your position, is difficult to fathom. Not very believable, I must tell you, and you must know that."

"I'm telling you, I am not and have not been aware of missing funds. Believable or not. I know nothing of this."

"Well, that will be your problem in explaining it. In the meantime, the bank will not be opening today. We will see about opening in the days to come. The gentlemen with me here are charged with securing the money in hand and ensuring nothing leaves the premises. A locksmith will be arriving soon to change the locks. Now, please locate Mr. Carroll and have him come here so I can serve this order of closure to him as President of the bank."

"Yes, sir."

"For the benefit of account holders, so that they know, the closure will be in force until further notice. We will do all we can to protect their deposits. Just get the President here, and I suggest you inform the employees they can go. They must not take anything with them, other than personal belongings. One of my men will be at the door to make sure of that."

"Will, what are you doing here? It's the middle of the afternoon." Maggie saw the worried look. It was all over him. He never came home this early. "What in the world has happened? You look like a ghost. Is it about Burroughs?"

Will had not shared with Maggie his suspicions about missing records, missing accounts, about the bank inspection of a few weeks before. He had wanted to spare her the worry. That would be over. "They've closed the bank, Maggie. Money is missing."

"What? The bank closed?"

"Yes, the inspector for banks showed up this morning, The officers of the bank are suspected of fraud. They served a closure edict, freezing all accounts, changed the locks on the doors. Burroughs apparently misdirected funds. Accounts with balances in the books but not enough cash anywhere to cover them. Ernie Carroll is in trouble, they think he knew and I guess, me as well. I could be arraigned."

"My Lord. You? Bank fraud? You can't be involved in this, Will. Huh?"

"Come on, Maggie. I don't know anything about it. They say the amount of money missing is close to twenty thousand dollars. Burroughs handled all the communications about the inspection of accounts. He kept me out of it. And, he insisted on keeping the books of the major accounts and deposits in his office, in his safe."

"Many times you told me you thought he was being secretive about things. But, Will…..your job? What are we going to do? There is no other one like it in Wamego."

"I don't know. All is happening so quickly. If what they say is true, people will never believe I was not involved. I'm the everyday number two man at the bank. How could I not know? I don't think the President or the other officers were involved. It's just not like them. But I could be charged. Even if I'm not, people will always believe I was involved. This is not good at all. And all those people who had their money at the bank. I'm not sure it will be protected." Will could not stop. The words continued to come out. "There is a surety that the bank took out years ago, but it may not cover everything. I don't know what I am going to do. People may not want to hire me. Whether I am absolved of any wrongdoing may be irrelevant. People will believe what they want to believe. I have been the everyday face of the bank for over fifteen years. I don't know."

Wamego Reporter, December 4 1919

FARMER'S BANK CLOSED. FRAUD CHARGED

He saw the headline. The content of the piece said it was believed that Ralph Burroughs, the deceased cashier had 're-routed funds to his advantage' but that there were no indications anyone else at the bank was involved. The article said there was a surety on deposits that had been purchased years before by the bank from the National Surety Company of New York. It was hoped that deposit holders would be able to recoup their money. Will could no longer get into the bank. The locks had been changed and the people from Topeka in charge of the closure were not giving out any new keys. He was locked out. He no longer had a job and wondered if he would ever get another one in Wamego.

A crowd of people had formed in front of the house. Men were yelling. Someone threw an egg. Others followed with more eggs and tomatoes splattering the door. "You're a crook, Will! You were part of it! Damn you. Mag, your plays are finished!" Mag and Will heard it all. Will opened the door to confront the crowd but got a tomato to his face for the effort. "I wasn't involved. I didn't know."

"A crock, Knecht. Damn you."

"The truth will come out. You will see," responded Will. In vain. Someone threw another egg, just missing him. He turned and went back in the house.

The next day....

"Don't tell me you weren't involved and didn't know anything about it. You were the damn assistant cashier!"

"I'm telling you, Hank, I knew nothing about it," said Will to the man who had confronted him on the street in front of the post office. He was part of the crowd at the house the previous afternoon. "May be difficult for you to believe, but it's true. And I feel bad for you."

"Impossible, Will. That nice car you have now, that house all spruced up, Mag going to Denver and Kansas City for shopping. We know all about it. Don't try to bullshit anybody on this. I lose my money and you're in trouble. And just about everybody else in town feels the same way. You may have a few more of what happened yesterday." The man who Will had known for years turned and walked away.

Maggie was upset, and had been ever since the closure. "Will, you didn't know about the money disappearing? How could you not know? Nobody believes you, and nobody believes me when I tell them."

"How many times do I have to tell you? I didn't know. I didn't have access to all the ledgers."

"What are we going to do? I can't go outside. Can't go downtown. Can't go anywhere. I walked into the post office this morning and everybody left when they saw me. The theatre group is finished. Lenora, Ethel and Helen quit. Said they would return if I stayed away. I said I would. They then decided they didn't want to revive it after all. Said it was all tarnished because of us. It's finished. What are we going to do? Our money is caught up in the bank like everybody else's, Will."

"I know. We're in the same boat. I tell them we are caught up in this also, just like them, but they don't believe me. They think we've got money stashed away somewhere. Even if they did believe me, they will think I'm a real dunce to have had this going on under my nose."

"Barbara called. It's all over the Topeka paper this morning – Burroughs' suicide, the closure, the fraud accusation. Said a couple of state senators talked about it at the house at breakfast. She wanted to know if we were going to be all right."

"What did you say?" asked Will.

"I said that we would. That you were not involved in the disappearance. That we would make it through it all. She didn't sound so convinced."

"Barbara has a nose for these things. She knows this could be trouble."

"Could be, Will!? It is. How could this have happened?" Without waiting for Will to respond, she turned and went the back door. Through the window, Will could see her walking down the back lane with arms rigid at her side and fists clenched.

Will did not find a job. Within six months, he had given up trying to find one in town. He tried Manhattan. Nothing. News travelled. His association with the bank was poison. Maggie feared for his health. He didn't know what to do with his days. He had sold the Chevrolet and had found a used Model T. It would have to do, but even then, he had little use for it. He had nowhere to go. Frances finished the school year at the convent in Salina. The fees for the year had been paid in advance but it was clear she could not return the following year. She would be going back to the parish school in Wamego.

Maggie had raised chickens for her mother on the farm when she was younger. She took it up again, with George building a coop and henhouse out back. She raised a flock of hens that laid a few dozen eggs every day that she would sell to Jimmy's grocery downtown. She also started baking pies for the grocer - cherry and apple. As many as two dozen a day. Jimmy's pies were so good, everybody said. There was no pie crust like them anywhere else. Few people knew that Maggie made them, and she wanted to keep it that way. George and Barbara helped out with money when she and Will needed it. Maggie was too proud to ask, but George could find out easily enough about their difficulties. Funds would be offered to Maggie, sometimes accepted and sometimes not, with no fuss or talk about it. Will would be kept in the dark. His humiliation had run deep. Nobody in the family wanted to deepen it further.

In the meantime, little Bobby was ever-present in the lives of the Tauers of Wamego. Maggie had him for days, sometimes weeks at a time. At two and a half years old, the little guy with the sandy hair that stood straight up, did not walk anywhere. He ran, everywhere and anywhere, chattering away constantly in a gibberish that only Frances seemed to understand. He got into everything, chased the chickens out back, got flour all over himself in the kitchen, 'helping Mag' bake her pies, and screeched with delight when Winnie or Frances would bring him a lollypop or some other piece of candy from the drugstore. "You're spoiling him," Mag would say. But she never took away the candy. What a joy this kid is, she thought. All these females looking after him. Spoiling him rotten. May it never end.

One day, she heard Bobby say something as he was playing on the floor of the kitchen. A pile of little wooden blocks had fell over. "Oh shit," he said. "Bobby, you can't say Oh Shit! That's a bad word. You should say Oh Shoot instead!" Bobby looked up at her and replied. "My Daddy says Oh Shit when we're in the car. I don't want to say Oh Shoot. I want to say Oh Shit, just like my Daddy." She couldn't help but smile.

Chapter 21

"Barbara, how long have we known each other?" William Adams, Kansas congressman for close to twenty years, now a Senator, was at the table in the corner and had motioned for Barbara to come over.

"Going on twenty years, I would say. First time we met was in Washington. The circus. I was with Mrs. Barnett when you came over to say hello. I remember Ruth saying I was from Kansas."

"Yes, she did say that and I remember it well. Then there was another time in Kansas City before you came back here. You found me ring-side seats for a large group of people."

"Then of course the many times over the years I've had this place. You were the first Congressman, I believe, to have dinner in our dining room. I've told you that before."

"Yes, you have. Who was I with that evening? I've been here so many times."

"Charlie Evans. Our dear friend the publisher, who I see often, by the way."

"Yes. Of course. One of many meetings I have had with him."

"He's here regularly. The Evans building is just on the other side of the Statehouse."

"He's come a long way. Biggest publisher in Kansas. Anyway, Barbara, I've got something I want to talk to you about, but we need to keep it between us. We've known each other long enough that I know you will understand."

"William, I understand. You know that. With everything I hear around here, I have to be careful. What is it?"

"The army wants to build an airbase here. Neither Fort Riley nor Leavenworth are suitable, apparently. The corps of engineers has identified a piece of land west of town that is apparently ideal for accommodating what the army has in mind. The government needs to buy that piece for the army to develop it."

"What's the property?"

"The one with the small landing strip on it, just off the highway, ten miles or so west of town. Cattle graze on it. It's a big piece. Ideal land for airplanes and all that."

"I know it and I know who owns it."

"I know you do. You know everybody. But here's my problem. Mr. so and so out there is a registered Democrat."

"Yes. I know," said Barbara. "And you can't have the government doing a major deal of the importance we're talking about with a Democrat."

"Exactly."

"So what do you want me to do, William? The man in the White House is a Democrat. It's a Democratic administration."

"It won't be for long. Wilson is incapacitated, and they can't win the election coming in the fall. Too much fallout from the League of Nations stuff and all. Could you set up a meeting between the owner and someone I have identified who could be the buyer?"

"Someone who is a Republican?"

"Of course. Just like you said, I can't have the government doing a deal of this size with a Democrat. Just not acceptable to our supporters here. But whatever is done regarding this, there cannot be any mention of me. Anywhere. I just want this investment for Topeka, for Kansas, with our local Republicans congratulating me for it. Not for arranging the deal but, as Senator, bringing the base to Kansas and to Topeka in particular."

"Bill, somebody buys the land and then re-sells it soon after to the government. Looks fishy, would you not agree?"

"There is no rush in this, Barbara. The army's plan is to have the airfield ready for use something like three years down the road. It will be hush-hush for a while. The purchase gets done, assuming the man agrees to sell, then a year later, the army says it has bought a piece of land that already has a landing strip on it, and no fuss is made. Nobody else in Kansas knows about this, by the way. The army does not broadcast these things. We can keep this very quiet. How do I know about it? Because I'm on the Senate military appropriations sub-committee. I get wind of these things. But I can't have the army fingering me for any leaks about this. Here's what I would like you to do. The owner who lives not far from here has dinner here once every two weeks or so."

"How do you know that?"

"My assistant tells me so. I asked him a while back to find out all he can about so-and-so. Anyway, what I would like you to do is call my assistant the next time the gentleman makes a reservation for dinner, let him know the date, and we will inform our potential buyer to have dinner at the same time. Then, when the gentleman shows up, he will ask you if Mr. so-and-so is present, and you will
136

say yes, and point him out to our faithful Republican who could propose a deal the man could not turn down. We would let the two men take it from there. That's all, Barbara."

"Why don't you just have your man go out to the property and get things started directly out there?"

"Because the owner is never out there and he keeps such a low profile. I don't think it wise for our investor to knock on the man's door at his place here in town, a very sumptuous place by the way. A little bit too direct. Need to make it more of a chance encounter. Your house here is the prime meeting place in town for anyone who wants to get things done. Influential people meeting other influential people. Mr. so-and-so would not be so surprised. Hopefully, a deal could be made. The airbase would come to Topeka and everybody would be happy."

"Alright, Bill. I can do what you ask. As a Topekan, a fellow Republican, and a friend of yours."

"I have no financial interest in this. I want to make sure you know that. I just want to make it happen. By the way, I may have a buyer for your shop. Is it still for sale?"

"It is. Haven't received a decent offer yet, but I would still like to sell. Is this part of the help you are asking me for?"

"Of course. I want to help you, because you help me."

"I will be glad to help with something that can come to Topeka."

Later that evening, over a late dinner with Tom, well after Bobby had been put to bed. "Saw you with Bill Adams," said Tom.. "Quite an operator. Earnestly in discussion with you."

"Yes, Bill is an operator. Always doin' favors. Been doing it for twenty years."

"What's he up to?"

"Bringing stuff to Topeka. Wanted to know if I knew somebody. I'll spare you the details, but he told me he may have a buyer for the shop. I thought I had somebody a while back, but no. Anyway, I hate going there every morning. I would much prefer to be the nanny to Bobby in the morning. By the way, you know that Bill Adams is half-Indian."

"Yes, I know. Part Seneca and part Pottawatomie. Only the 2nd congressman in the history of the country who is Indian, even half-Indian."

"He knows how to take care of those people."

"He has the clout."

"Tom, I have a thought. Bill knows so many people. Maybe he could help Will find a job. Companies looking for people with financial experience. Will wasn't involved in the fraud in Wamego. That has come out now, thank God. Just the same, he's wallowing down there. Maggie is selling eggs and making pies every day to make ends meet. Maybe Adams could help."

"Maybe so. Talk to him about it."

The next morning Barbara crossed the statehouse grounds and found Adams's office up the street on the opposite side. The Senator was about to leave for a meeting, but had Barbara come in. "Bill, I agreed to do you a favor. I need one from you now."

"What is it? Will be glad to help if I can. I was serious last evening about knowing someone who could buy your shop."

"It's not about the shop. My brother-in-law, husband of my dear sister Margaret in Wamego, was the assistant cashier at the bank there that had to close because of embezzlement by the cashier, who took his own life by the way."

"I remember that. Sordid affair."

"Well, he was cleared of any wrong-doing. The bank inspector confirmed that publicly. But people in Wamego don't believe it and nobody wants to hire him. He needs a job. He's a good man. Could you think of someone who may be interested in hiring him? He's been in banking for fifteen years. Could most probably work on the financial side anywhere. His name is Will Knecht."

"Sure. Let me see what I can do, Barbara. OK. Will Knecht. I'll be happy to do what I can. I gotta run. Let's speak soon. And thanks for accepting to help with the airbase issue."

"Not a problem, Bill. Have a good day."

Three weeks later, William Adams was back from Washington. He was at a table in the rooming house dining room. When he saw Barbara in the doorway, greeting other guests as they came in, he motioned for her to join him. As she approached the table, he asked her to sit down, then made sure no one else was in hearing distance. "Barbara, your brother-in-law Knecht. I can't help him, and I'll tell you why. He systematically over the years turned down just about every loan application from the Pottawatomie when he was at the bank. Apparently a pattern. Your sister's husband doesn't like Indians. And that causes me a problem."

"Oh." Barbara could see that this was not going to work.

"You must know, as most people do, that I am Indian, one quarter Pottawatomie. I have spent my entire life working to better the lives of my people along with those of all citizens of the state and the country. Anybody who is an enemy of Indians is an enemy of me. I am not going to help your brother-in-law. That is unfortunate, as I have learned that your sister Margaret is much loved by the people on the reservation. She just happens to be married to someone I cannot help. I'm sorry. This will not affect my respect and admiration for you, Barbara, nor do I hope you hold this against me."

"My Lord. Systematic rejection. I'm sorry, Bill. I had no idea. I don't think my sister does either. The Pottawatomie – an elderly blind lady from the reserve, to be specific – cured my little boy of a horrible rash he had when he was a baby. I am grateful to them. I'm sorry about my brother-in-law. I understand. I thank you anyway for looking into it. Hopefully, we can stay friends."

"Oh, we will. Just sorry I can't help. It's too much for me," replied the Senator.

'Maggie, we need to talk. Just you and me."

"What's it about, Barbara?"

"Not on the telephone. Too many possible ears on the line. It can wait 'til we see each other, but we must talk."

"I'm coming to Topeka on Saturday. I want to see Bobby. Taking the train. We can talk then."

"Alright. I'll be at the station. The train arrives at 12:30 if I remember. You can stay overnight."

"OK. See you then."

Barbara greeted her sister at the train station and soon got into the taxi. Maggie looked over at Barbara. "Where's Bobby? And where's Tom? He couldn't drive you here?"

"He's at the shops today. They work Saturday mornings and he has to stay for awhile and make sure everything is wrapped up for the weekend. And Bobby's at the house with the nanny."

"You're still having him being taken care of by a nanny. I knew it would be this way. He should have a full-time mother. I would have been a better mother for him."

"Mag, let's not get into that."

"It's not right. Louise would be furious. I should have been the one to take him."

"With an unemployed husband and you making pies all day. Some mother it would be for that little boy."

"You're being so mean, Barbara. You always have to win, don't you? Bobby's so happy when he's with us in Wamego."

"Listen, Mag. I invited you here to tell you something."

"Ok. What is it?"

"I asked Bill Adams, our longtime Congressman and now Senator and a friend, by the way, if he couldn't find something for Will. He knows a lot of people all over the state. I thought he could help. You know of Bill Adams and you must surely know he is half-Indian. I asked him if he could find something for Will. Well, he came back to me this week and told me, as a half-Indian and Pottawatomie to boot, that there was no way he could help Will. Told me people on the reserve said that Will had turned down just about every loan application the reserve had made over the years. Systematic rejection, he said. One for a road and another for a new school particularly got him upset, he said. And because of that, he was not going to help find him a job. Said he was sorry and hoped it would not affect our friendship. He did say, however, that you were much loved by people on the reserve and was sorry he had to deliver the bad news."

"What? Will systematically turning down applications from the Pottawatomie? He never told me anything about that."

"I don't suppose he would," said Barbara. "So don't give me trouble about Bobby. I have tried to help you two. In more ways than one. I have offered to take Frances here to Topeka and put her in the fine school here, but you said no."

"Well, I'm going back home. We've had the discussion. You've told me what you wanted to tell me. I need to speak to Will and I don't feel like waiting." Maggie was upset. She leaned forward and said to the driver "Turn around. Take me back to the station. Please."

She turned back to her sister sitting next to her in the back seat. "Barbara, this doesn't change my feelings about Bobby. I appreciate your attempt to find a job for Will. Right now, I'm just so mad."

"You don't want to see Bobby?"

"I'll see him some other time. When you bring him to Wamego. I'm going home."

Chapter 22

"My Daddy hated Indians. He fought them when he first came here. There are some things I never told you about my father."

"This is not about your father. It's about you, God damn it, Will, and your attitude about Indians," responded Maggie.

"Well, I have to tell you these things anyway. And hold back on the cussing. One is about a cousin of his, something he saw with his own eyes. He was seventeen or so, riding out somewhere west of Abilene with his cousin and others, and his cousin was caught by Pawnee after a chase when his horse stumbled. They killed him. My dad saw it, hiding in trees up a hill. Said it turned him against Indians forever. He told us about another incident, again something I never told you about. A member of Dad's family from Germany who went further west than here, back in the 1850's when the family was still in Pennsylvania, was killed along with his wife and son by Comanches. Dad didn't know them, he was too young, but his father told him about it after the killing of his cousin by the Pawnees. Dad railed against us kids having anything to do with Indians. He would have nothing to do with them, no matter if they were Pottawatomie, Seneca, Kaw, Osage, or any other. Forbid us kids to talk to them. I told you that when we were kids."

"You did, but you never said anything about family being killed."

"No. I didn't. We were not to talk about that. I knew you had friends on the reserve, so I never said anything."

"That's what drove you to refuse all those applications?"

"Yes. When I went to work at the bank, Daddy made me swear that I would never have anything to do with Indians there. It was my part of the deal for him to have his friend the president hire me. Said he would disown me if I ever helped an Indian. Repeated the stories of his family."

"The Pottawatomie never hurt anybody here in Kansas, Will!" Maggie was upset and shook her finger in Will's face as she spoke. "If there's a tribe that has tried to live alongside us whites, despite all the prejudices and the cheating them of their rights, it is them. The most docile and respectful of any of the Indians of Kansas. I can't believe you did this, Will."

"They're Indians, Maggie. That's what they are."

"If I was not such a devout Catholic, Will Knecht, I swear I would consider leaving you. Consider yourself lucky. What would you possibly do without me? Damn it, Will. I can't believe you have done this!" She rose up, walked around the table and came back to stand in front of her husband. "I don't blame William Adams for refusing to help you. You deserve it." Maggie then turned, went out the back door, and walked down the lane towards the park in the middle of town. She found a bench under one of the big elm trees and sat down. There were children playing.

I have always put out of my mind that Will despised Indians. He's known my feelings. Probably why he never told me about any loan applications or anything having to do with the reservation. He never wanted to go with me there, even when we got Kewanee's mother to treat Bobby. I sensed it then, but I didn't say anything. I should have. Who is Will after all? I've known him all my life, but I feel I don't know him. Was he so ignorant of what was going on at the bank? Is he so innocent? Is there something I don't know? Something the town knows that I don't?

Maggie's thoughts turned to other things as she watched the children chase each other around the big trees. Bobby. How I love that little boy. Louise would be proud. He would be blessed if she was still here, but he'll never know her, and he'll never know she is his real mother. Maybe it's just as well he is with Barbara. We will soon have no money. Things will be difficult. I will have to look after Frances, who was doing so well. Bobby. Doesn't look like Louise. More like that damn father of his. Such a shame. Insane. May he never show up to take him. God forbid.

She looked off to the left past the children playing and saw Helen, her partner in theatre of years past with her daughter walking towards where she was sitting. At that moment, Helen saw Maggie and abruptly turned to walk in the opposite direction. Everybody avoiding me. Even Helen. We may have to leave here. …Can it be? After a few minutes, a thought came to her. No. We won't. I'll prove them wrong. The full truth will come out and Will will be absolved. I'll do it. She got up, crossed the park, reached their street and noticed the car was not in the lane next to the house.

After Maggie left, Will drove out to see his father, who lived alone on the big farm. Will's mother had died many years before. His brothers and their families had their own houses on the large piece of land. "What are you doing here?" his father asked as Will came around the car and approached the big veranda.

"Came to see you."

"Somethin' bothering you, right?"

"Yes, Dad, something is bothering me." He had decided on the way to get right into it. He walked up the steps and leaned against the post in front of the rocking chair. "Why did you turn me against Indians and so many other people?"

"I told you, they killed my kin, your kin. Dirty savages. Don't deserve to be alive. None of them are any good. Too bad you're married to an Indian lover. And, about other people, before you get mad, Will, I always told you to look after yourself, and to hell with everybody else."

"Well, that's what I did and look what it got me. Maggie despises me now. I'm hated in Wamego. I may never get another job around here."

"I got you that job at the bank and you messed it up."

"No, you messed it up for me. That loan I got for you. Burroughs blackmailed me over it. Got me to agree to let him do what he wanted. It has ruined me, Dad."

"Shut up and bear it, Will. You've got no backbone."

Will looked at his father, turned and went down the steps to the car, and drove away. It was the last discussion he would ever have with his father.

Chapter 23

Looking through the framed glass door leading to the guest parlor and what used to be the living quarters of Mr. and Mrs. Hagen, she saw him. Down the hall opening every door and looking in before moving to the next. A customer looking for something? He was oddly dressed for a customer – wool shirt with no jacket or waistcoat. She then saw the broken window in the solarium. Not a customer. An intruder. As she turned to find a telephone, the man came back down the hallway shouting "Where is he? Where is my son? Where is everybody?"

"Mrs. Hagen, this is Maria. There is a strange man in the guest parlor, rummaging around and yelling. Looks like he got in through a window in the solarium. The window's broken. What do I do?"

'What is he yelling, Maria?"

"Something about his son, and where he was."

Good Lord. Amos. He's escaped. "You go to a room and lock the door. Tell any guest you see to go to their room, that there was an intruder, and that the police would be arriving soon. I'm calling them now. Mr. Hagen and I will be there soon." Maria knew nothing of Amos Muller, that he was Bobby's father, certainly nothing about the boy's true father being in a mental institution. Employees as well as all other people Barbara knew were told that she had adopted an orphan and that the child's parents had died soon after his birth from the deadly flu that had ravaged the country. Maria would now wonder if the story about Bobby was true. She would have to speak with her. No one who worked at the house made the connection with Louise, who used to work there before any of them did. No one needed to know that her little Bobby was her sister's son.

The police captain addressed Barbara as she and Tom entered the hallway. "Mrs. Hagen, he's holed up in a back room. The door's locked. He says he has a knife and will use it if anybody tries anything. We've been waiting for you to get here before we storm the room. He's incoherent. Ranting something about a son, how he was stolen from him."

"Let me talk to him. I think I know him." She knew him of course, but she didn't want the whole city police department to know what this was all about. "Can I do it without everybody hearing what we have to say? In the meantime, you should call the mental hospital and ask if anybody is missing. And if so, get a team over here to take him back."

"Why the state hospital, Mrs. Hagen? You think he is from over there?"

"I think he is a former customer here. I heard he had been committed. Just in case, get them here. I think he is one of theirs."

"Alright, but I can't let you get close to that door in there. Let us speak to the hospital first, and then decide what to do."

"Get Barbara Tauer here! She has my kid. I'm going to find him and take him back! He's my boy!" It was loud enough for the police captain, the two officers with him, and Maria to hear it. Barbara looked at them. "Get the hospital people here. The man is delusional. He somehow imagines he is the father of my son. I think the man is the former customer here who was so taken with
148

the little boy last year. He declared he would love to have a little boy like him. I heard later that that man was declared insane by the state and taken in by the hospital. I think it's him."

Four men dressed in white arrived soon afterwards. Two policemen accompanied them to the room where Amos had locked the door. One of the policemen rammed the door with his shoulder, the door gave way and the policemen soon managed to immobilize Amos, despite his size and strength. The hospital staff put a straightjacket on him as well as a bandana around his mouth and carried him out. He looked at Barbara on the way, mumbling through the bandana, trying to free himself from the straightjacket. They got him into the hospital wagon and drove away. The police captain approached Barbara. "He is Amos Muller, Mrs. Hagen. He was married to a Louise Tauer, who I understand is your sister."

"Was my sister. He caused her death. I have his son, through a judge's order that was never made public. I would appreciate it you would be discreet about this, Captain. My employees and all but a few people in Topeka are unaware the boy's true father is Muller and a man declared insane. I need to keep it that way."

"I want to see one of your residents, Amos Muller."

"Ma'am, this is a bit out of the ordinary. We don't often receive visitors for our patients. When we do get requests, we nevertheless try to accommodate." The nurse at the reception desk hesitated before continuing. "It may be a problem to see Mr. Muller. I take it you are family?"

"People come here and they are just forgotten? Nobody comes to see them? They're gone. Is that it? And yes, I am family, if you must know." Quite apart from her motivation to come and see Amos, Barbara was appalled at what she was hearing....and seeing.

149

There was no joy in the place. No pictures on the walls, no color anywhere.

"Unfortunately, that is the case with so many of our patients, but I will say no more about that. In any case....Mr. Muller. Although you say you are family, I must ask who you are and why you want to see him."

"He is my brother-in-law. He escaped from here last week and tried to find me."

"Yes. The incident. I have to tell you Mr. Muller is in confinement."

"Can I see him? I need to talk to him."

"I'm afraid that will not be possible."

"Will it always be that way? You just lock them up and nobody can see them?"

"No, it's not that way. Listen…..Mrs…….."

"Hagen. Barbara Hagen. And I would like to know when I can speak to Mr. Muller. I insist."

"Wait here. Let me speak to the administrator."

A few minutes later, the nurse returned. She was with a bespectacled middle-aged man in a white coat.

"Mrs. Hagen, I understand you want to see Mr. Amos Muller."

"Yes, I do. I am his sister-in-law."

"You must know that Mr. Muller is a dangerous man. He can be violent at the slightest provocation. He is in quarantine at present."

"I know that, but I must speak with him. When can I do that?"

"I will see what we can do. We will inform you."

Two weeks later, Barbara received a call from the hospital. "You can come and see Mr. Muller. He has agreed to see you. He will be accompanied to ensure your safety. Please come tomorrow at 10 AM."

"Thank you. I will be there," replied Barbara.

"Syphilis, Amos. My Lord. Why didn't you tell her?"

"Go to hell, Barbara. I agreed to this meeting to talk about my son, Aaron. How is he?"

"He's fine. But his name is not Aaron and you know it. Louise named him Robert before she died. His name is Robert. Now, why didn't you tell Louise about your condition? She knew nothing about it."

"I didn't want to lose her. And I don't want to talk about it."

"Well, you will, whether you like it or not. You knew she could die."

"No, I didn't."

"You mean you didn't know the effects of the disease? Did you ever see a doctor about it?"

"No, I never did. I got over the sores. I thought it was over."

"You knew you had it, Amos, and you did nothing. You are despicable."

Amos rose up and lunged across the table. The two men in white were quick, preventing him from reaching Barbara who had recoiled, with her chair nearly toppling backwards to the floor.

"Damn you, Barbara Tauer! I will get back at you! Beware! I am coming!" The words streamed out as the men dragged Amos out of the room. Barbara could hear him yelling all the way down the hall. One of the hospital administrative staff came into the room. "This went badly. I thought you would be more kindly with him, Mrs. Hagen. I'm afraid we can't do this again."

"I'm sorry. I could not contain myself. He caused the death of my sister. I will not ask for a visit again." With that, Barbara rose and left the hospital, getting into the taxi that had been waiting for her, never to return.

Chapter 24

In 1921, two years after the bank closing, the Wamego Reporter published a story saying that the state bank inspector's office had been made aware that Will Knecht knew something was wrong with the accounts but did nothing. There was no indication of how they found that out, but it did say there was no evidence that Knecht had taken any money. The contention was that he had simply remained silent. The story said the inspector's office would not comment as to whether Will Knecht would ever be allowed to work again in a bank in Kansas. With this report, Will retreated further into melancholy and anger. He spent his days essentially doing nothing, reading the newspaper, going downtown where people including old friends avoided him. Maggie's hell continued. She retreated into church work. Her days filled with organizing church-related activities and with pies and eggs and the supplying of such to Jimmy's Grocery on Main Street. Weekends with Bobby were welcome breaks of happiness. George and Barbara were kind to Maggie and helped her out in whatever ways they could. George paid for Frances to go with Winnie to a summer camp for girls in Minnesota. Barbara offered to take Frances in for her to be able to go to the Topeka Catholic high school as opposed to the public one in Wamego. Maggie's financial burden would be less, but she refused the offer. It was a source of acrimony between them.

"Mag, you're acting out of pride. I'm doing this out of goodness to you. Can you not accept it, for once?"

"Barbara, I will look after Frances. She will be fine."

"Still smarting about Bobby. Will you just get over it?"

Maggie looked at Barbara and said nothing. There was a tear in her eye. She looked away, then said with her back to her sister "Let's not talk about it, Barbara. Frances will be fine in Wamego."

"The case is closed, Mrs. Knecht. I cannot share the file with you. By state law, all details of banking investigations are sealed. There was fraud, as we said in the judgment. The details were shared with the state attorney. The person who perpetrated the fraud was identified publicly."

"Ralph Burroughs. And nobody else?"

"Nobody else, Ma'am. We determined that the President of the bank was not aware of the diversion of funds. There was no proof that anyone else was either."

"You say no proof. Nobody else involved."

"We could find no evidence of anyone else being involved."

"Could the inspector of banks publicly say that the other officers of the bank were not involved? People in Wamego believe my husband was part of it. Could you publicly clear him of any involvement?"

"We don't do that sort of thing. It would never end if we did. We have stated that Mr. Burroughs, the cashier, was responsible for the diversion of funds and we will have to stick with that in terms of any pronouncements. You must know that most depositors have received their money back through the surety bond the bank had with the banker's trust company in New York."

"Not everyone. And whoever did get money back did not get back all of what they were owed. And my husband cannot get a job in Wamego or anywhere else for that matter because people believe he was involved. Had to be in on it, they say, and no one wants to confirm officially that he was not. His life, our life, is being ruined because of it."

"I'm sorry, Mrs. Knecht. I can't do any more for you."

"How was the meeting in Manhattan?" she asked. Will had walked in the door and came into the kitchen. Maggie was rolling the dough for another set of pies she would deliver in the morning, just like every morning for months.

"They were being polite. I had helped them out with a big loan a few years ago, for a plant in Salina. I had gone to Mr. Carroll for them, to make sure the board would approve it. They knew that. Just the same, they hemmed and hawed about the job. They were being polite. They're not going to hire me."

Maggie said nothing and continued rolling the dough, flattening it out, cutting it into round pieces to place in the pie pans, then trimming the edges. "Those envelopes over there, Will," she said as she worked. "One is from Daylor. He says we owe him eighty two dollars for work they did on the Chevrolet. The second one is from the insurance company telling us we are late on our premium for the year. Do we have money for these, Will? I don't think we do." It had been five months since a paycheck. They had lost half of what they had with the bank. What they would recover had still not been refunded by the receiver.

"We don't. I will have to work something with Daylor, and the insurance. They will have to wait."

"Letter says we must pay within thirty days or the policy will be cancelled. And something I have not shared with you, we can't continue to take money from George and Barbara. George paid the last fee from the convent."

"I may have to sell the car. And George and Barbara have been giving us money? I didn't know that."

"Lots of things you don't know. Yes, they have. I resisted at first but have relented. It's how we've managed to survive." As she always did when making her pies in the summer, she raised her hand to her face, her finger catching the sweat that had accumulated on her chin, then flung her hand towards the floor with a rapid flip of the wrist. Spots of sweat were everywhere on the floor. She was concerned about something else, something she would not tell Will about. At least not yet. She had received a call from Lucille Burroughs who wanted to meet her about a matter. She would see what it was about.

"Maggie, I found something in Ralph's papers. It has to do with Will. I must tell you this. It's not something you would want to hear, but I have to tell you."

Mag tensed up. She liked Lucille. They had always gotten along. She had felt sorry for her for having to put up with what she thought was such a distant, aloof husband. "What is it, Lucille? What do you have?"

"Ralph kept a journal. I did not know he did. It was in a box in his closet. I never really went through the stuff he had in there. There were boxes of papers from previous jobs, old bills, cancelled checks. Well, I decided I'd better get into it. The bank inspector asked me to look through any personal papers that they had not found on their own. I said I would and would give him anything that had to do with the bank. Maggie, I will have to turn over the journal. There is an entry in there about a favor to Will. You're not going to like it."

"Tell me. What was it, Lucille?"

"Ralph said in the note that he would approve a loan for Will if Will promised to not insist on going into the ledgers he had in the safe. As Cashier, he had the right to refuse anyone else looking at them, except the President. "My responsibility. Will Knecht acknowledged that," are the words in the diary. Maggie, I don't know if Will was aware of what Ralph was doing. I have been appalled by it all. It has ruined my life. I just thought I should inform you they will have this, and it could be trouble. They had some deal, apparently. It doesn't mean he knew what Ralph was doing, just that he would not probe. I'm sorry, Maggie, but I thought you should know."

My God. He knew, and he agreed to keep quiet about it. A loan. What loan?

Maggie walked into the house and saw Will, seated in the living room. "What was the loan for, Will? The bank loan you never told me about?"

"What loan?"

"The one Burroughs approved that you never told me about. What was it?"

"Where did you get this? Who told you of a loan?"

"Lucille. She told me she found a note in Ralph's papers at home that she will be obliged to turn over to the banking authorities. The note said that Ralph approved a loan to you in exchange for you not insisting on seeing the stuff he handled. To facilitate the orderly, efficient management of things, he said in the note."

Will hesitated. Maggie was upset. It would be futile to try to put her off. He stood up, went around the table. "Ok, if you must know, it was for the Chevrolet."

"You're lying to me. You traded in the Model T for the Chevrolet with Daylor and paid the balance from our savings. You showed me. What was the loan for, Will? And for how much? Don't lie to me."

"I told you. It was for the car."

"A load of crap, Will. What was it for, goddamn it?!"

Will leaned down, put his hands on the back of a chair, hunching his shoulders, then spilled it. "It was for Dad. He owed a lot of money to someone. Bought a bunch of cattle to supply the army and couldn't pay for them. He had lost his contract. The war was over. They didn't need the meat."

"You never told me that. Why didn't you, Will?"

"I just didn't. Dad was humiliated. Caught. He made me promise not to tell anyone. The bank refused to give him a loan to cover it. They already had a long-standing mortgage on the farm. The old president was a friend of Dad, the new one, Carroll, was not. I decided to help him."

"And do you still owe the bank? To repay the loan?"

"Yes. But the bank is bankrupt. It's closed."

"But whoever owed the bank, still owes the bank, don't they?"

"Yes, they do."

"Well then, is the bank receiver after you?"

"How do you know about bank receivers?"

"I read the papers, Will. The bank stuff is all over the paper every week. Notices about receiver this, receiver that, people getting their money back or not. Is the receiver after you?"

"Yes, he is. But we have no money and I told him that."

"He could take the house, couldn't he, Will?"

"Yes, he could."

"Well, have you heard from the receiver on this?"

"Not recently."

"When was the last time?"

"Three weeks ago."

"How come I've not heard about this?"

"All correspondence is with Sullivan, the lawyer. It all goes to his office. I wanted to spare you the worry."

"Well, I'm not spared, Will. What in the hell are you going to do? What are WE going to do?"

"I don't know."

After supper, Maggie said she was going for a walk. She went to see George, whose house was not far away. There was no way she was going to share this with Barbara. She had enough problems with her sister. She told him about the loan, the threat to seize the house. "What can I do? You know something about these things, George. You are in business. Loan foreclosures, all of that."

George was not surprised. He had always thought Will was too ambitious, not careful with his money as well. He hesitated a moment, then asked "How much is it for?" Maggie told him. "I will take care of it. I don't want to see you go down. If you lose the house, you will. You've had enough grief and hardship. There is money I have from what Poppa left us. I invested it. It's there. It's family money. I was the oldest son and inherited it, but it's family money. I will pay off the loan."

"Are you sure you want to do this?" asked Maggie.

"Yes, this is for you. But Will will not go scot-free. I will tell him he has to work for me a number of hours a week, until the loan is repaid. Half of what he earns will go to him, the other half I will keep to pay off the loan."

"He's not going to like it. He has never done manual labor."

"Well, he'll just have to get used to it. He's still a young man. I never told you this, but a few months ago, I offered him a job. He turned it down. Said he could never work as a carpenter. He didn't want me to tell you that. I should have. I didn't know about the trouble with this."

"Yes, you should have, but I am grateful for what you want to do. I will make him take it. If he raises a stink, refuses to do it, I will tell him I am leaving him, marriage vows be damned."

"He's lucky to have you, Maggie. I'm sorry this is happening to you."

"I married him. We have known each other since we were kids. He was always my man. I'm not happy these days. But I have to look out for Frances. I won't leave him. I couldn't bring myself to do it. I will threaten him with it, though."

"You and Louise both deserved better. Much better."

"I can't work with George. Doing carpentry and all that? I can't. I've never done any of that stuff."

"Well, you'd better learn. It's the deal. George bails you out, you go to work for him for as long as it takes to pay him back."

"I won't, Mag. I'll find another way."

"There is no other way. Nobody is going to give you any money and nobody other than George is going to hire you. You know it. And, if you don't take this offer, Will Knecht, I will leave you."

"You will leave me?"

"Yes. You have deceived me. I will leave you. So, it's up to you. You take this or I am gone, and I'll bring Frances with me."

Will got up from the table, walked to the back door, stood there for a moment, then turned around "Ok. You win. I'll go to work for George, damn it."

"It's not all. You knew. Knew about Ralph."

"I suspected. I didn't really know. I didn't want to."

"You better hope this doesn't come out in town. The banking authorities will have the information from the diary."

Will crossed the floor and leaned back against the counter in front of the table. "I never took any money like Ralph. All I did was accept to not question him about stuff he kept in his office. You know it now. From what you tell me, that is all the note in the diary says. I was stuck, Maggie. I had to stay away from his files. It was the arrangement I had with him. He said some of the accounts were 'commercially sensitive' for Wamego and were better kept strictly confidential. I agreed to it, and I shouldn't have."

"You better hope the banking people don't view that as illegal or somehow part of Ralph's operation."

"I suspected things. I could have looked into them, but I didn't. I wish I had, but Ralph had me. I thought he was doing some special deals for some businessmen, keeping them hush hush, away from Carroll and his cronies in town, not skimming money for himself. Does George know anything about what was in Ralph's journal?"

"No. I didn't tell him that. Only about the loan that you have to pay back. Never again, Will. No deceiving me ever again. Understand?"

"Alright."

"George is waiting for you to talk about what you are going to do."

Will would work for George for three years to pay back what he owed. It was a rocky relationship and it ended as soon as Will had paid back what he owed. Will Knecht was not a carpenter or construction guy and would never be one.

Gradually, Maggie's friends came back to her. They observed her work with the church. They saw how hard she worked on making ends meet. They saw how Will was so disconnected, melancholy, angry. One day, two of Maggie's old friends showed up at the house. Mag answered the door, with flour on her hands and her apron.

"Hello, Mag. Can we come in?" asked Helen at the front door. She had been a close friend and a steady hand in the theatre group years before. She was not alone. Two other women from the group were with her.

"Well, yes. Come in. I was in the middle of making my dough for today."

"It's been awhile, Mag," Helen said as the ladies sat down at the kitchen table amid pie plates and egg cartons. "I'll get straight to the point. We want to resurrect the group and we want you back. We're sorry about how we've treated you." The women looked at Maggie. There was a moment of silence. "We want you back. Can we do it?" Maggie hesitated, then with tears beginning to form, looked up at her three old friends "Yes, I think we can," as she wiped away a tear.

"We're sorry. We have been so unfair to you. What Will did was done. It's over."

"You girls are making me happy. You don't know how much I have needed this." Tears were running down her face. All three women got up, walked around the table to Maggie and hugged her. "You're getting flour on your clothes, girls."

The first play of the renewed Wamego Playhouse Theatre Group opened four months later, in October 1923. It was sold out. The play, a comedy, with Maggie playing the lead role and cracking jokes throughout the piece, ran once a week for two months. By Christmas, plans were complete for a spring production of another comedy, which would evolve into a series concerning a bumbling, yet infectious farm couple and their family. Although Margaret Knecht would still be making pies and delivering eggs to the grocery, her dignity was back. And the little boy who was often with her made everybody smile, no matter where it was. On the street downtown, at the Post Office, after church on Sunday, wherever. She would bring Bobby with her to the theatre when he was in Wamego. At the show on the first weekend, the little guy, six years old and sitting in the front row with Will, George, Mary and Frances, rose up as the curtain opened and cried out while pointing at Mag "That's my Aunt Maggie!" The scene stopped immediately and everyone in the audience laughed. Frances promptly leaned over and dragged Bobby, with by now a sheepish look on his face, back into his oversized seat. Mag and everybody else on the stage were smiling. Their nervousness had evaporated, and the show went on.

In the five years that followed, apart from the two plays from the comedy series they put on every year, Maggie and Helen wrote four plays, three of which were taken on by the Denver theatre agent and published. Several theatre groups from New Hampshire to Oregon ran their comedies, originating from the initial series about the bumbling Kansas farm couple. They started receiving royalties. The amounts were not great, but they were something. Maggie Knecht had always wanted to be someone of the theatre. By the summer of 1927, she could truthfully say she was one, and not just in Wamego, Kansas. Then, there was the radio. It got started with a telephone call.

"Mrs. Knecht, my name is Jack Miller. I am a producer with radio station KCKO in Kansas City, part of the Radio Mutual network. You may know of us."

"Well, I have heard of Radio Mutual. What can I do for you?"

"I understand your theatre group where you are, it's Wamego I believe, does some interesting comedy. I am told your comedies are popular, people enjoy them, and are being played in theatres around the country. We would be interested in seeing if they could work for radio."

"On the radio? Our plays? We do them on stage."

"Yes, you do, but they could perhaps be put on radio. Could we talk about this?"

Maggie had difficulty believing what she was hearing. "Mr. Miller, I'm stunned. We never thought of that. But I would be glad to talk about it."

"Very good, ma'am. When is your next production? I want to see one of them."

Maggie thought for a moment. A repeat showing of one of their most popular productions was scheduled for Saturday, ten days from then. "The next show in Wamego is Saturday night after Labor Day. I suggest you come and see it, judge for yourself if it could work for you."

"Very good, Mrs. Knecht. That would be a good start."

Barbara drove Bobby to Wamego the following weekend. Maggie told her about the phone call. "Mag, I know KCKO. It's Kansas City's most listened to station. I also know the owner. This could be great for you."

A week after the show in Wamego, Maggie received a contract from the station. A one hour show every two weeks for four months per the scripts submitted, to be extended at the discretion of the station. Two hundred dollars per show, plus travel and lodging expenses. The letter said the name of the show would be the Sunflower Comedy Hour, and that hopefully the first eight shows would prove to be popular enough that the series continue.

"Where are we going to get the material?" asked Helen.

"We have it already. All we have to do is continue the Mom & Pop series. Make it an on-going affair. That's what Jack Miller saw when he was here. We have enough material for it. We can do it."

Chapter 25

Charles Evans was the owner of the biggest media organization in Kansas. He owned the Topeka Herald-Journal, the main Topeka radio station and another in Kansas City. He owned the largest newspaper in Wichita, and ten smaller ones across the state. His printing company was the biggest in the Midwest, with plants in six states. Evans had his preferences for Kansas politicians who were involved in national politics and he wanted to play a role. Having friendships with governors, state legislators, members of Congress and municipal politicians around the country helped his businesses. Evans was aware that Barbara had known the governors or lieutenant governors of at least half the states. She also had met the mayors of many of the largest cities in America in her years with the circus and had maintained contact with many of them. He knew she made sure those people were told where to stay if they ever came to see anybody in Topeka. Keeping the contact information of people she had met in her circus years had served her well for that business and now served her well in her business in Topeka. Through the ownership of the rooming house, she was a connector for influential people. Although Barbara relished the influence, she kept it as low-key as possible. Not many women could claim the same. When they did, men managed to knock them down. "Just ask Eleanor Roosevelt," said Barbara once when someone brought it up.

Topeka was important in those days. Kansas was Republican and in the first decades of the century, produced some of the most influential operators in the national Republican party. The state was also home to the highly influential newspaper man, William Allen White, editor at the Emporia Gazette. Charlie Evans and Bill Adams were among a select group of people who could call White at any time and discuss their views on matters of the day. Barbara never got around to doing that. It would have been a bit too presumptuous, but whenever Mr. White was in Topeka, he had lunch at the Hagen House and made a point of having a few words with Mrs. Hagen.

Adams, Evans, White, the state legislators who frequented the house, had always been amazed at how many people Barbara Hagen knew and how she worked the dining room. Sitting there one day, waiting for a business contact to arrive, Evans thought of Ernesto Perez, the rich Venezuelan living in Texas, who Barbara introduced him to a few years earlier. She said she had met him in Florida, when visiting Ruth Barnett in Palm Beach. An oil man. Said he wanted to get in on the oil boom in Kansas. Got him in to that, he thought. Barbara had the governor facilitate the granting of drilling rights. Said it would be good for Kansas. Foreign money being invested in Kansas. Managed to get him rights for fields near Hays, Humboldt, and McPherson. Amazing. Then the deal for the radio stations in Texas. Could not have done it without Ernesto's money. All because of Barbara. What a woman. Knows more secrets in this town than anybody over there, he thought, glancing at the elegant Capitol building across the street as he walked back to his office. Now wants to talk to me about corruption. Washington. Alright. She knows a lot. And her sister. What a gal, my guys tell me. Sunflower Comedy Hour. One of our most popular programs.

Since returning to Topeka and opening her businesses, Barbara had become active in several issues, both local and national. She was active in the one to give women the vote and rejoiced when Congress passed the 19th amendment in 1920, giving women the right to that. She had organized a delegation of Kansas women to Washington that year. She was also active in supporting Prohibition, as many women were at the time, but later turned against it, believing it contributed to criminal activity. It was an issue that would be front and center in politics in America throughout the 1920's.

American political affairs in those years were dominated by scandals and reports of corruption at the highest levels of government. The news was full of it every day. Bill Adams knew a lot of what was happening in Washington and didn't like it. He was the Majority Leader in the Senate. "Need to get the bad apples rooted out," he told Barbara. "Ruining the reputation of the party." But he had to be careful. He could not be identified as a source of inside information. The Harding administration was Republican. His party. How could he get things into the media? The answer came quickly. Barbara Hagen. Friends with Charlie Evans. Got to talk to her.

"Where did you get this, Barbara?" Evans was astonished. There was enough in what he was seeing to bring down a cabinet member.

"I can't tell you. All I can tell you is that the letterhead of the memorandum speaks for itself. You will have to do your own verification, Charlie."

"Head of the Veterans Bureau taking money from contractors. Internal memorandum inferring exactly that. This is quite something."

"Harding and his people are blind. The people should know. I may be a woman, and nobody wants to listen to somebody like me. What do we know about things? Well, I know a lot and I am really upset about this one. I have a nephew who lost a leg in the war. He also has shrapnel in a lung. The hospital that was supposed to be built for Kansas veterans is not being built. This probably has a lot to do with it. I'm doing something about it."

"Where did you get this?"

"I told you, Charlie. I can't tell you that. You will have to do your own digging to back it up. It's all I can do. Do with this what you believe you should. I believe you are a Republican, Charlie. If this continues, the Democrats will be back in and soon. Have to stop this stuff."

A month later, the Veteran's Bureau scandal broke. According to a story in the Wichita Eagle, owned by Charlie Evans, the head of the bureau who had been appointed by President Harding was accused of skimming millions of dollars from contractors. The man had fled to Europe in advance of the story and the bureau's chief legal counsel committed suicide in the week after it broke.

A few months later, the deputy Attorney General of the United States was charged with taking money from bootleggers to evade prosecution for violating Prohibition – the selling of whisky on Indian reservations - and Charlie Evans was talking about it. His newspaper in Kansas City had broken the story, and his radio stations broadcasted it. It was national news. Bill Adams had provided the information to the paper through an intermediary. Barbara knew it but did not tell anybody she was aware of how the information had gotten to the Evans Company. "Charlie, I am not surprised this is going on. Prohibition has led to these things. Criminal activity, corruption of officials. I have turned against it. Kansas can be all for prohibition, but I'm against it now. Just leads to more trouble than it's supposed to solve. Here's something you may want to publish." Evans never learned that Bill Adams was behind the information implicating the Washington officials. He never knew that Adams had told Barbara he was incensed there were people in the government facilitating the sale of booze into native communities. The entry of alcohol into reserves was worse than it had been before prohibition. Adams was determined to see an end to it. For him, if Prohibition was to work, it had to work first and foremost on the reserves. Alcohol was killing his people. And, for Barbara, it was killing the people who had cured her little boy, something she never forgot.

Chapter 26

Barbara feared that Amos would come to take Bobby. When the boy was three, Barbara convinced George to let Winnie come and help look after the boy. She would go to high school in Topeka and was happy about it, even if her friends were back in Wamego. Her aunt was somebody in Topeka and she knew she would have a better chance for a more exciting life than in the country. The rules for Winnie were that if Bobby was outside, she was to be with him and not lose sight of him at any time. She would take him for a walk every afternoon after coming home from school. When she was to take Bobby downtown or to the park, it had to be with someone else, most usually the neighbor's teenage son. Every other weekend, Tom and Barbara would take Winnie and Bobby to Wamego, where the boy would stay with Maggie and Frances, who would take over from Winnie in looking after him. When Bobby was five, he was given responsibility for looking after the chickens, a duty he was proud of. "I don't break eggs, Aunt Mag. I'm a good manager of the hen house," he proudly said one day. "Bless your heart," Maggie would say, something she would often say over the years.

While Bobby was growing up, he would refer to his two female cousins as his fairy godmothers. "Where are their wings, Bobby?" someone would ask. He would say "They don't need them. They're pretty enough they don't need wings and they're not make-believe."

One day in 1921, when Bobby was four, Barbara received a call from the state hospital. "Mrs. Hagen, I have to inform you that Amos Muller has escaped from the hospital again. We are looking for him and the police are involved. We don't know where he is, however. He somehow escaped during the night."

"How could that happen? My Lord. I thought he was in a secure part of the hospital. You know of the threats he has made. This is very worrisome."

"I know and I'm sorry. But right now, I urge you to take precautions. He may show up."

"He will definitely show up! I cannot believe this. I am going to call the police. I will have them put somebody here. I can't live with this over our heads. Is there not some way to have Muller taken in elsewhere? He is being held in the same city as us."

"I'm sorry, Mrs. Hagen. This hospital is the only mental hospital in the state. We would have to send him to another state and that is not easy. I'm sorry."

Barbara hung up the phone, then called Tom at his office. "Tom, Amos is out again. We must get away from here. Go to Wamego, maybe somewhere else. He knows Wamego."

"I'm coming home. We'll take him to Lawrence; stay in the hotel for a couple of days until they find him. We'll have to do something with Winnie. She can't stay at the house if we are not there."

"You're right. Maybe we can go to George's. I don't think Amos ever saw his house. He will not know where it is. Winnie will be OK there. She'll be home. And Albert is there. Amos would have difficulty dealing with Albert. Hopefully, they can find him, for God's sake. We can't continually be on the run from that man. I

172

asked them why he must be at this hospital. They say there is no other place for him in Kansas."

"Ok. Wamego at George and Mary's. I'm leaving now."

Two days later, Barbara called the state hospital and found the administrator. "I'm glad you called, Mrs. Hagen. I tried to reach you at your home, but there was no answer. We found Muller. We have him."

"Well, that's good to hear. I hope you never manage to let him out again. Quite unacceptable that he can do it. He's a dangerous man. He has threatened us, and you will remember the scene at our rooming house two years ago. Where did you find him, if I may ask?"

"In a tavern in what everyone calls Little Russia, the neighborhood down along the river. He had robbed someone in uptown and was spending their money. The police had to subdue him. He had a knife and could have used it. He's back here now."

Little Bobby spent a big part of his younger years in Wamego. When there, Frances would take him everywhere she went. She had a boyfriend who played baseball and would take Bobby to the games down at the park on hot summer nights. The three of them would then get a root beer at the hot dog stand afterwards. "I am going to be a pitcher one day and strike out all those big mean guys from Rossville," Bobby said. "You watch."

"Oh, you're gonna have to practice, Bobby," said Dale, who was Wamego's first baseman. "How are you gonna do that?"

"I'll find a way" said Bobby. "I'll find somebody to throw to." "

"How old are you?" asked Dale of the boy with his legs dangling underneath the table.

"Five," he replied.

"OK. You talk a lot for five. Anyway, you find a way to practice throwing and I'll go see you on Saturday and see how you're doing."

The next morning...

Mag was aghast. "Bobby Hagen, what are you doing!!?" she yelled through the screen door. She had heard a couple of 'splats' and a loud squawk from the chicken coop in back. She was now observing Bobby throwing eggs at the rooster from the bowl he used to collect the morning eggs. The boy froze and looked back at Mag coming towards him. "Little man, you are in trouble! Give me those eggs! Get in the house! What are you doing?"

Bobby looked up at Mag with a frown on his face and the beginning of tears in his eyes. "I was just practicing my pitching with some extra eggs, Aunt Mag. I want to be a pitcher and I don't have a baseball to throw."

"In the house! You can't do this, Bobby Hagen! No more collecting eggs for you. And no ice cream tonight or tomorrow night. Baseball! What has Frances got you into? In the house!"

"You are in trouble," said Frances a few minutes later, finding Bobby sitting in the chair on the front porch, sulking at the dressing down. "You can't be throwing your Aunt Mag's eggs at the rooster or at anything. She needs those eggs to pay for the groceries. She's very mad at you."

"I just want to become a pitcher like that big guy from Rossville. Dale said he would come to see how I'm doing. There were six more eggs than usual this morning. I didn't think it would hurt."

"Well, you'll have to become a pitcher another way," she said, standing over Bobby, who had sheepishly reclined as far as he could in the big chair. "Now, you come with me. Mother says you will have to help me with cleaning up the upstairs. Now!"

"Where's Bobby?" asked Mag an hour later.

"Well, we finished cleaning upstairs," said Frances. "And I told him to take the wastebasket to the trash can out back. He's around somewhere."

"Around somewhere. Well, I called out for him and there was no answer."

"Maybe Dad took him down to the depot."

"I don't think so. Dad left a half hour ago and Bobby wasn't with him. He always tells me when he has Bobby go with him. I should not have to remind you that you have to look after him, Frances. That's your responsibility when he's here."

"That little rascal. I'll go look for him."

Ten minutes later, Mag was in the kitchen and through the screen door saw Bobby enter the henhouse.

"I thought I told you to stay away from the chickens, Bobby Hagen. What are you doing now?" she asked as he exited and ran right into Mag's skirt. She could see he had a small box in his hand with the grocery store lettering on the side.

"Well, I went to the store and got you some eggs and put them back in. To replace the ones I broke. There will be more to pick up in the morning. I'm sorry, Aunt Mag." He had tears in his eyes. He dropped the box, which Maggie could see was empty.

"You went to the store and bought some eggs and put them back with the hens? Where did you get the money?"

"The money I get from the lady across the street for bringing her mail to her from her mailbox."

Maggie bent down and hugged the little boy. "Bless your heart, Bobby Hagen." She took Bobby's hand and walked to the house. "I think we'll have to find a way to get you a baseball."

In 1924, Barbara officially adopted Bobby, whose real name on his birth certificate was Robert William Muller, but who had always been known to everyone including the people at his school as Robert Hagen. Barbara had explained that to the parish school when he started in the first grade. The school complied with her request. She hoped that Amos would never come back and claim the boy. Given his condition, she knew that was never likely to happen, but she worried about it anyway. Nevertheless, Barbara used the clause in the agreement with Muller that if he did not manage to pay within seven years what she was owed for the care of Louise, she could adopt the boy. She did it as soon as the seven years were up. Barbara was thankful that Bobby had never brought up that he had heard his last name was Muller. He never did. She was pretty sure that he had never heard it. The nun who was the principal had kept her word.

In the meantime, Amos Muller did not try to escape from the hospital. Barbara never saw him again. In 1925 she learned that he was transferred, at his request she was told, to an institution in Pennsylvania, where he was from. She never heard from him or about him after he left the state of Kansas.

Chapter 27

February 1928...

"Bobby, you know Mr. Adams. He is our Senator in Washington. This is James, who works with Mr. Adams. He'll be eating dinner with you here in the kitchen."

"What's a Senator?" asked the ten-year-old.

"An important man. He looks after Kansas in Washington."

Barbara left Bobby with Bill Adams's assistant and returned to the dining room to be with her guests.

"Momma has dinners for all these people, but I have to eat in the kitchen. And I get the wings. The only chicken pieces I ever get to eat are the wings. It happens every time. Why does anyone have to look after Kansas in Washington?"

Barbara's guests that evening were Senator Adams, Charlie Evans the publisher, Jay Hoak, the mayor of Topeka, and Bud Krause, director of the Kansas Republican Party, along with two state senators. Tom had begged off as he knew what the dinner talk would be. It would be about politics and he would just as well avoid it. None of the men's wives were present. Barbara had told her guests it would be a 'working dinner'. Most dinner parties at Barbara's were with men and their ladies, but this one was different.

Charlie Evans spoke first, after the initial course had been disposed of. "Ok. We all know what this dinner is about. Barbara has been kind to bring us together. We have the opportunity to run Bill here as Hoover's running mate. He could do it. We all know it. Bill, we are talking about you here, that's for sure and I know you are a humble man, so I invite you to just listen, at least for awhile while we go over what we think." Turning back to the others, he continued. "Bill represents the reformer wing of the party. Nobody else has his credentials in that regard. And Hoover needs a running mate from the heartland. Kansas has never had a vice-president."

The discussion went back and forth as the men discussed how they could position Kansas' favorite son to be on the presidential ticket. They all knew that Bill would first have to submit his candidacy for president. It was not too late for that. The convention would almost certainly select Hoover as the nominee. William Adams would concede, then, hopefully, there would be enough support at the convention for him to be selected by Hoover as his running mate. They and other allies in the party would work to make that happen.

Bud Krause, the party man who had known Adams longer than anybody, spoke up. "Bill, do you want to do this? Go with Hoover? He's not easy. He's clean in regard to the corruption things that have dogged us, but he's a strange fellow. How do you see it? It's going to be up to you in the end."

"I know what you guys may be thinking, despite everything you have said. You have been very kind, and I am flattered. But the Indian stuff. It may be too much to overcome. You know my story on that and you know my record on doing things for them. A lot of people have not liked that. Many people in America are prejudiced against Indians."

"Bill, your record in the Senate is beyond reproach. Only the party radicals, the bigots, of which there are many we all know, could blame you for anything. There are the isolationists as well. They are influential and we must beware. Teddy would have never allowed us to advocate abdicating our international responsibilities. Too bad he's gone now. He would have run again and I dare say would have probably selected you for his running mate if he had. All in all, Bill, you would be a moderating influence on Hoover. Most importantly for him, you could deliver the Midwest."

"If he would listen to me. Vice-presidents don't have much say."

The discussion went on for another two hours over the rest of the dinner of baked chicken (without the wings), mashed potatoes, creamed corn, boiled stuffed tomatoes and biscuits, Barbara Hagen's favorite dinner menu. Most dinners in Kansas usually featured beef. It was Kansas. But at Barbara Hagen's, it was always chicken and always the best chicken dinner served in town. Barbara loved being the hostess. She did not always get a word in but loved being at the center of politics in Topeka. She never told people what went on at her dinners and her guests knew it. There were people in the legislature who believed she knew more about what was going on in the state than anyone. And when someone important needed a favor, a word passed on, they knew that Barbara could probably deliver. But she had to keep quiet about it.

Barbara instilled in Bobby a curiosity about the world. She had travelled to a lot of it, at least to the European and American parts and wanted to make sure she shared her knowledge of them. She spoke to him about history and about how things worked in the world. She talked to him about war, his cousins Albert and Leo in the Great War, his grandfather's cousin, Franz, the cavalry officer in the paintings in the living room who had been destroyed by his own war so long ago. She told him about how people had been mean to Germans in Wamego just a few years before – the Tauers were of German ancestry and his grandfather, her father, had a heavy accent. His Dad was Irish, and his Mom was Bohemian German. She also gave him a sense of ambition, of the need to excel, to go beyond, to do good things. Tom backed her up, demonstrating the best of being a responsible hard-working father and husband.

Back in the kitchen that evening, Bobby struck up a friendship with James, twelve years his elder, someone he would run into much later in life. They talked about baseball. James had met Babe Ruth; had also met Jack Dempsey, the boxer, and had both of their autographs. From that evening forward, Bobby Hagen told himself he would meet as many famous people as possible and collect their autographs.

Tom had walked in as the discussion was ending. "Gentlemen, I hope you have had a good discussion. I won't ask you what it was about, but I think I know it was somehow about politics." With a wry grin and nodding to his wife at the end of the table, he continued. "I will say no more, but I do invite you to join me in the parlor for a cigar and a glass of brandy."

"Where were you, Tom? You didn't have any dinner?" asked the Senator.

"Oh, I had dinner. At the Knights of Columbus hall, where they have a great chef now. You know me, Senator. I am not involved in politics and I don't want to be, so I wasn't here. But I do like a glass of brandy and I hope you will join me."

Later, after the guests had left. "You are amazing, Barbara. You manage to bring these men together and get them talking. I saw their faces. They looked to be a happy bunch at the end of the evening."

"They are. We are going to get William on the ticket with Hoover. At least we have the genesis of a plan for it."

"Right here. The plan for a vice-presidential run, right here from the Hagen house in Topeka. I'll say it again. You are amazing, my dear. Where did you get the wherewithal to do all this?" asked Tom

"I've told you many times. The circus. Ruth Barnett was quite an operator. She knew everybody and made allies and friends of all of them, and sometimes had me doing the busy-bodying, certainly having me know what she was up to. I saw it all. I guess it rubbed off. And maybe growing up in New York with other immigrants. I went to school with Italians, Jews, Poles, other tough Germans and Czechs and, I must say, devilish and scheming Irish. Survival. Smarts. I don't think I got any of it on the farm. I was bored, couldn't wait to get away. Spent too much time in the hustle and bustle of New York. Anyway, my dealings with the people here tonight are all about connecting people and being discreet about it. I can't run for office. Women don't do that; not yet at least. I guess I've found a way to get involved."

Six months later, at the national Republican convention, Herbert Hoover announced that William Adams, the Senate Majority Leader from Kansas, would be his vice-presidential running mate. Bill Adams would be the first man of significant Indian ancestry and the first man from Kansas as well, to be nominated as candidate for Vice President of the United States.

Chapter 28

The KCKO Sunflower Comedy Hour show of March 1930 was its last. The sponsors had stopped paying. The series was over. Maggie and Helen and three others from Wamego who formed the usual cast had been occupied with the series virtually full time for over two years. The 1929 contract paid them five hundred dollars a week and the comedies were heard throughout the Evans radio network, from Kansas City and Wichita to Joplin, Missouri, to Lubbock and Waco, Texas. Other stations in Arkansas and Oklahoma had contracted in September to start in April. But the adventure was over. The crash happened in October and troubles had begun for everyone. Maggie and her troupe nevertheless decided to continue, bringing the series back to the Wamego theatre, renamed for the purpose the Wamego Sunflower Comedy Playhouse, with a first showing in May. The radio shows were adapted for the stage, and admission was twenty-five cents. Despite the low cost of admission, the series struggled. Money was tight in Wamego. The series closed the following April, when the last show had only twelve people, the one before that only fourteen. There was not enough revenue to even pay the building heat and light bill.

Mag was back to baking pies and selling eggs. Frances managed to keep her job with the optometrist, allowing the bills to be paid. Will did not work. He spent his days lamenting his condition, arguing with most everyone he encountered on his daily trips to the train depot or the café on Main Street. The depot was where the unemployed men of town would congregate on the outside benches and share stories of their days and complaints. Mag managed to ignore it all. Her focus was most often on Bobby who continued to spend many of his weekends, as well as long stretches of summers, in Wamego. He would spend time with Frances and Winnie when she was home from college, as well as with neighborhood boys he would renew with every summer. July 4th celebrations were special. The fireworks in the park. The best in Kansas, people would say. The swimming pool, where he learned to swim. Lake Wabaunsee where Will on his good days would take him fishing. Catfish and perch. Perch was good, the catfish not so good, he would say. And Albert and Leo. They would take him fishing as well and, in the fall, take him rabbit hunting in the fields around Westmoreland.

Maggie remembered the time when Bobby was eight and it was a few weeks after Halloween. Halloween had been over and done with, but he found a clown's get up in the attic in Topeka, from Barbara's time with the circus, brought it to Wamego, and went to the old men's boarding house in town. He insisted that Frances take him. He went there at dinner time in the clown's outfit and did a number in the dining room, just like the one he had seen at the circus Barbara took him to in Topeka. He put on a show, as Frances told Mag. "Those old people could use a laugh, and I can provide it. Just like the clown in the circus," he had told Frances on the way there. Bobby did a pantomime, repeating as best he could what he remembered from the circus he had seen a few weeks earlier. Everybody clapped. They were all surprised. No one had ever done something that before. He finished the pantomime, bowed and then went skipping out the door. A couple of men came out and gave him a quarter before he and Frances got very far up the street. Frances told the story of the evening for weeks afterwards to people who came to the optometrist's office.

Maggie also remembered the time a few years later, when Bobby was eleven and back in Wamego for the summer, when he got the 'meanest old fart in town' to back the boys' baseball team to allow it to go to the big tournament in Wichita. Will Parsons, 'that mean old scrooge who had bought the drugstore' was reputed to be the richest man in town, and Bobby zeroed in on him. The baseball team needed a sponsor to pay for their trip as well as for uniforms. 'The old ones will not do', said Bobby and went after the old man. He went to see Parsons and told him he could be the 'Pride of Wamego' and loved by everyone for allowing the boys to bring a championship to the town. "We're good, Mr. Parsons. Nobody around here beats us. We can win it in Wichita. And you can be the man who did it. I'll get my uncle to make up a banner and put it up over the drugstore for all to see. That you did it. You made Wamego proud."

"The old meanie did it," she told a friend from Manhattan later that summer. "Paid for new uniforms, got them a couple dozen new bats, paid for the bus ride and George put up that big banner. Parsons kept it up there for a year. Bobby had sucked him right in. His mother, my good sister Barbara, couldn't believe it. Anyway, the coach said when I saw him just before they left, 'That kid will go a long way.' And I'm sure he will."

Here we are in distress with this national condition, thought Maggie, this horrible disaster, with just about everyone going broke, and he shows up and lights up everyone around him. He laughs. He jokes. He pulls a prank. He does it all the time. When he was little, the time when he was five when he hid Will's shoes. Said he would bring them out if Will brought him for an ice cream cone. I cry. He lights up our lives. Ever since he was a baby. Louise would be so proud.

Chapter 29

Bobby didn't like the attic. Dust and cobwebs and old things. He was looking for his old wooden rocking horse. He wanted to give it to the little boy next door. He found it in the corner behind a chair with a covered box on it. As he moved the chair aside, the box fell to the floor, the cover came off and a pile of papers fell out. As he picked them up to put them back, one of the folded documents caught his eye. Written on the back cover were the typewritten words "Agreement between Amos K. Muller and Barbara Tauer Hagen concerning the care of Robert Muller, minor, June 16, 1917." Robert Muller…Who's he? he thought. He unfolded the document and began to read.

He went downstairs. Winnie, visiting, was in the parlor. Nobody else was home.

"Winnie, I found this in the attic. Look at this and tell me if you know what it's about. Mother agreeing to look after a boy born to Aunt Louise, who I never knew."

Winnie looked at the words on the cover. She opened it up and went through it quickly. She didn't have to read very far. She knew what it was about. She looked at Bobby and realized she would have to tell him. Barbara must not know about this. "Bobby, let's go back upstairs. Your mother can't be aware you have found this. Please. She may come in." They went up the stairs to the attic and closed the door behind them. When they reached the attic, she had Bobby sit down on one of the dust-covered trunks at the top of the stairs. He stared at the floor, not looking up. Winnie reached down, took his chin in her hand, and made him look up at her. "Bobby, you have to swear to me. You will never tell your mother you found this. You must never let her know. Your father either. Will you swear that to me?"

"Yes. And I think I understand." He looked at his cousin. "Robert Muller is me. Is that true? Winnie?"

"Yes, you are Robert Muller."

Tears welled in his eyes. "And Mother is not my real mother." He was choking on the words. They had difficulty coming out.

"No, she is not your real mother, Bobby, but she is still your Mom."

"So, my real mother is Louise, who died, and my real father is the man in this document. Amos Muller. Is that true, Winnie?" A tear rolled down his cheek. He swept it away with his hand.

"Yes. Your mother who brought you into this world died soon after your birth. The mother you have known all your life took you and adopted you."

"What ever happened to my father, this man, Amos Muller?"

"We don't know. He disappeared."

Bobby looked at Winnie, tears in his eyes.

"What was she like? Louise. Did you know her?"

"She was a wonderful person. Kind, generous, loving, a beautiful woman as well. We all loved her. She would rock me to sleep when she visited us. Told me stories. Frances and I loved her. Albert and Leo did too. Everybody did."

"What did she die of?"

"Childbirth, Bobby. It happens."

"My father. You say he disappeared. He just left?"

"I don't know what happened to him. Nobody knows. Maybe your mother knows, but I'm not sure. He was probably distraught at the death of your mother. He is no longer around. No one has seen him for a long time."

"How old was I when she died?" Booby asked as he wiped away his tears with the back of his hand. "When my real mother died?"

"You were a baby. The date of the paper you have in your hand is less than a month after you were born. She died just a few days after your birth. Your mother Barbara took you as her own. She made the arrangement with your father."

"What was he like? My father?"

Winnie hesitated a moment. She wanted to be careful. "He was a nice man. I hardly knew him, but he was nice to me, and he loved your mother. Barbara took you in to help him. He had no way to take care of you, and he owed people money. He owed Barbara money. It's there in the document in your hands. Your mother paid all the bills for the care of Louise. It was not a situation for a man to be able to take care of a baby."

The boy was silent, looking at the document. His life had just been turned upside down. His parents were not his parents. Winnie took him in her arms, held him. "Bobby, listen to me. You promised me not to tell your mother. Do I have your word? She would be devastated. She has been your mother all your life and that should not change. She loves you more than anything. Do I have your word?"

"Yes. You have my word. I promise. She will never know." He backed away, wiped the tears from his cheeks, then stood straight and looked at Winnie. "Mom will always be Mom." At that moment, they heard the front door open. Barbara was back. They left the attic and went down into the hallway, where Barbara saw them from the bottom of the stairs. "Well. You two have reunited." She saw that Bobby was red-eyed as she went up the stairs with a package. "You're all red-eyed, Bobby. What could that be about?"

Bobby looked at Barbara and responded quickly with a smile. "The dust in the attic. I was looking for an old toy. I kept sneezing and rubbing my eyes. Winnie came up to help me find it."

"What was the toy you were looking for?"

"That little wooden rocking horse. I want to give it to little Davey next door. He has so few toys."

"Ok. You sure you're Ok? Must be a lot of dust up there."

"Yeah, Mom. I'm fine."

Chapter 30

September 1936....

She was sitting alone on the porch. It was a hot sultry late summer night, with the sound of crickets and cicadas punctuating the silence of the evening. Her thoughts were on her life, on Bobby, her sisters, the family.

Bob... gone back to college last week. What a young man. He is so good to me and so good to Mag. A special relationship with her, like a second mother. A third, really. She dotes on him, just as much as I do. Louise, God Bless You! You made a great son. That bastard of a husband of yours. You deserved so much better. But what a boy you produced. In California now; best he's there. St.Mary's is a good college, just like the Archbishop said. He has the scholarship. He's supposed to play football and did last year but got hurt. He shouldn't be doing it. He's really not big enough, but he says the coach wanted him back. High school was one thing, but playing Nebraska and Stanford is something else. He says he may drop it, but then we will have to cover the tuition and everything. We'll do it if it comes to that. He is doing so well and seeing so many other horizons. Kansas in this damn depression. The dust bowl. California is his salvation and it's good that Albert and Leo are not far away. Winnie is there as well, with that wonderful guy she met. But Bobby - so interested in the larger world. He talked my ears off all summer long. He gave those talks at the country club. Amazing. He got the manager to let him use the conference room to explain what the New Deal was all about. Gave conferences Thursday evenings after the pool closed. Knows all that stuff. He'll get into politics. That's what he tells Tom. He's always loved talking with Bill Adams, who rolls his eyes when he tells me about their discussions. He's got me believing in going Democrat now. For God's sake. Me, a woman of Kansas and a budding Democrat, although I can't tell anybody, not yet any way. Bill is amused by this. He detected my sympathy for the other side last week. I said it was all because of my son. In any case, they are going to be in charge for awhile. FDR is doing good things and Hoover messed things up. Big Bill was VP and had a good run. He managed to do a lot, despite the president.

Bobby said what did it for his interest in politics was when Roosevelt was here in '32 and he managed to shake his hand. That photo of the convertible with FDR and Bobby leaning on it. The jaunty hat and the long cigarette holder. Bobby beaming. Then, the next summer, going to the Boys State jamboree in Wichita. Over a thousand boys, from all over. Got him all fired up. He says he knows more fellows in Kansas now than anybody else in the state!

Mag. Mag. Mag. My lovable sister who has had it so rough. And Will - such a grumpy old bore. Resents that George and I have been giving her money. It grates at her as well but she manages to swallow her pride. They cannot survive on pies and eggs and it's getting worse. The grocer told her he would have to pay her less. The depression, he said. Folks having a hard time. But so resilient and a playwright for God's sake. Comedy and humor despite her situation. Too bad the show had to close, but she is so mobilized now. Really got on me last week. Roosevelt this, Roosevelt that. Says that Republicans didn't give a damn about ordinary people. Why couldn't I use my circle of friends for a better cause? Why couldn't I become a Roosevelt Republican? It would be difficult. Kansas is so conservative and just about everybody at the State house would disown me. Maybe I'll do it in secret, gradually. Anyway, I am not so influential or connected anymore. It was a good run, not bad for a woman who's not so pretty and never was. All because of Ruth. She showed me the way.

Ruth, my dear friend and benefactor. The letter from her niece saying she had passed away. At 84. She got me into all this. It was the spark, the chance to get out of Kansas. I would have never been able to do all this. What did Bill tell me the other day? An elderly man came up to him and told him he was once the deputy mayor of New Orleans. He said 'there was this big woman from Kansas – you're from Kansas are you not, Mr. Vice-President? – who was with the circus that stood up to the mayor who took no gruff from any woman. She told him where to go when he demanded extra free tickets and almost beat at him with an umbrella! Are they all like that in Kansas?' he asked. 'Barbara Tauer! That's who it was and I know her well. She still doesn't take any gruff from any men,' Bill told the gentleman. He tells me I'm a tough lady. 'A real mean squaw' he said. It could only come from William Adams, the nation's most famous Pottawatomie.

Chapter 31

May, 1937....On the train from San Francisco to Topeka.

Dad is so steady. Our fountain of wisdom. I don't know how he keeps up with her, though. Such a motor of activity. He's calm while she erupts. Lets her get away with running everything. Mag says I get my ambition from her and my down to earthness from him. They are not even my Mom and Dad, but they will always be that anyway. They will never know. How that upended me. That day, the discovery. It took a while to get over it. Lord, did it ever... Thank God Winnie was there. I would have made a real mess of it. Mom not my real mother and Dad not my real father. I wondered for a long time afterward what really happened, why Louise died. Winnie finally told me. Last year. I insisted. I told her I had found another piece of paper and showed it to her. A doctor's report. She gave in. I'm sure Mom had forgotten all about the paper. I never saw her once go up to the attic. Secrets put away forever, she probably thought. 'From the effects of transmission of venereal disease,' it said. But I will never tell her.

The train rolled through the scrub and desert of Utah. Bobby could see the table rocks of the badlands off to the north. St. Mary's and sophomore year over now, he thought. Great place, great guys, great teachers, all of them. And all thanks to Albert. Twenty-two years older than me but still my cousin. Got me to

California that first summer. Then the job at the Ambassador hotel. Mom got me that; knew the general manager who booked events around the country for the circus in her day. What a summer and what a place. Movie stars and all. The autographs. Bing Crosby, Jean Harlow, Eddie Cantor, James Cagney, Tommy Harmon, Max Baer, PeeWee Hunt, the band leader. F. Scott Fitzgerald who wrote The Great Gatsby. "Can I have your autograph?" So easy. James started it that time we were in the kitchen for dinner when everybody else was in the dining room. I probably have more than him now. But he's on to big things. Switched sides. Now working for Roosevelt. Mr. Adams is probably not happy about it, but he was fed up with Hoover at the end...told Mom as much. Mom will always be a Republican at heart. Kansas to the core. Mag's the Democrat in the family. They go at it. Mag's got the upper hand now, with all that Roosevelt has done. It was fun meeting him that time in Topeka when he was running the first time. Got his autograph. That huge convertible and the longest cigarette holder I've ever seen. Dad took that picture. He was there but Mom wouldn't come. She couldn't be seen with him, she said. Then the dinner a few days later with those guys dumping on Roosevelt. 'Communist' I overheard from the kitchen. With the wings once again. Mom could never handle beef. Gave her stomach ache, she would say. So...it was always chicken. Mag, too, but that was different. She had them in the back yard. Best fried chicken in the state.

What a gas, my aunt Mag. I may have lost my true mother, who I would so much have liked to know, but I have two other moms. Found a picture of Louise. So pretty. Winnie told me she was the prettiest of the girls, and that Maggie and she were close. Mag. What a sense of humor, a love of life, spontaneous joy at any time, despite what she has gone through. Uncle Will is no fun. For anyone. I don't know what really happened to him. Mag does everything, keeping things together. What a woman. The theatre, on the radio before everything crashed. They still talk about it in Wamego.

When I'm working and making some money, I'll help my Aunt Mag. Put her in touch with important people in the theatre, farther than Kansas. I'll get her going again. She is not that old. All those people I met at the Ambassador – somebody would know who to see. I'll find a way to reach them. We will bring back the Sunflower Comedy Theatre.

As the train rolled along, Bobby thought of his summers after Los Angeles, the hotel and the famous people. The Boy Scout camp in Arizona, the hike down the Grand Canyon. Mom wanted me to see it. Said she had never been. That summer when I was twelve before the Crash, and before I found that stuff in the attic, when we went to Chicago, Niagara Falls, and Quebec. Quebec! What beautiful girls. Incredible. They were everywhere.

Then the crash. Mom had all those stocks, and they went to nothing. Dad said he knew it was coming. He didn't believe in the stock market. It was a sham, he said. There were arguments about it in the car on our trip. He said she should sell it all. No, she said. No, no, no. She said that I should become a stockbroker when I grew up. I would make a lot of money. I didn't know what that was. What did Dad say a few months later? "I told you so." She walked away from any mention of it. "You're damn lucky you have the rooming house," he would say. "And you retired too early in '25" she would say. "You didn't have to." The arguments went on. Thank God she did have the rooming house. Legislators still need a place to stay. But Dad is the one with the financial discipline. Mom's not bad, but Dad is the conservative one. He hates to spend money. Talks to me about insurance now.

He looked out at the highway next to the track. An old Ford truck piled with chairs tied to mattresses, a Chester drawer, bags and a suitcase tied to the roof. A boy's face through the windshield as the paths of the train and the truck crossed, the family in it taking whatever they had left to hopefully make a new life somewhere else. The exodus from dust. He thought of the family down the street from Mag's. The father who used to work for George, dying one day. A surprise for everyone, Mag said. He had four small kids. His wife lost the house not long after that. The bank took it over. He had no life insurance and no other family in town. They just up and left. Life insurance. Even Mom doesn't have it, according to Mag. Said she bragged about having all those stocks, 'her real life insurance' she said Mom would say. I never really asked her. Mag says I should get into it after college. Dad talks about it too. 'Help people protect what they have, protect their family.'

His thoughts turned to the secrets of his parentage. Amos. My real father. I don't want to see him. Ever. What a sonofabitch. Winnie telling me he tried to come and get me when I was little, then disappeared. Nobody ever saw him again. I found him, though. I know where he is. Dauphin, Pennsylvania. The census of 1930. Amos K. Muller. 'Patient' at Dauphin County Hospital for the Mentally Ill. The one of 1920 listed him as Inmate, Topeka State Hospital. Took a while for both, but I found them. Mental hospitals. Winnie is not aware I know all this. No need to. In any case, I never want to see him.

The next day, Bobby arrived in Topeka and took a taxi home. Told his Dad he would do it. No need for him to get the car out and drive to the depot in North Topeka. "You're 76 years old, Dad" Bobby said on the telephone the day before leaving California. "No need to do it. I can darn well take a taxi. See you and Mom when I get there." As the cab drove down the street, Bobby could see the long white car with the red cross on the side and the open doors in the back, parked in the driveway. Something wrong. My God. Dad. 76.

He got out of the taxi, ran up the porch steps and into the house. It was not Dad. It was his Mom. She was on a wheeled stretcher. Doctor Nelson, who lived next door, was bent over her. So were the ambulance attendants. One of the attendants was trying to take a pulse, shaking his head. Tom came to Bob, trying to shield him from getting closer. The doctor looked up at Bob, at Tom, then back to Barbara who was not breathing. He leaned over, put his ear to her chest, then probed with his stethoscope. He looked up and shook his head. "She's gone, I'm afraid. Looks like a heart attack, Tom. All signs lead to it. There's nothing we can do. I'm sorry." On hearing that, Bob pushed the ambulance attendants in front of him aside, took Barbara's head in his hands, bent over and put his face to hers. He kissed her forehead, with his hands clasped to the sides of her face. He kept them there for a long moment, with his face close to hers, then rose up and turned to his Dad behind him; they shared a glance. Bob couldn't look at anyone else. He turned, found the front door, and went out to the front porch. Tom followed him, caught him by the elbow and turned him around. They hugged each other. "She's gone, Dad. She's gone." Tears were rolling down his cheeks. "I didn't have the chance to say anything to her. To say goodbye. To thank her for being my mother."

'Why did you have to thank her, Bob? She was your mother. Your mother. Period."

"I know, Dad. I know. What happened? Was she sick?"

"She was OK as far as I could tell. Nothing today. Nothing at all. No signs of any trouble. She was a bit overweight, she always has been. Stout, the doctor would tell her. She was always worried about heart attacks. Her mother, your grandmother, died of one when she was in her early 60's and that bothered her. She was in a great mood this morning. Was so anxious to see you. She had gone to the country club yesterday to make sure you had the job for the summer."

"I'm having difficulty with this, Dad. I never thought of her not being here. This is going to be tough."

"I know. It'll be tough on me as well. She took up so much of my life."

At that moment, the doctor came out, followed by the ambulance attendants. "Tom, there is no point in going to the hospital. The boys can take her to the funeral home, if you wish. It's a hot day. She shouldn't stay here much longer."

"Yes, the funeral home, of course. The one on Eighth Avenue is where she should go. The owner is a friend of ours. Bob, we should go and make the arrangements. Best if you come with me. Not sure I can drive right now."

"There was no sign of anything amiss. She had that energy. Always organizing something," Tom said as they drove the few blocks to the funeral home. "She was getting involved in the mayoral race coming up. What else. Always somehow involved. She had a meeting here last night over dinner, with a couple of people pushing their candidate. She said she would work to get him elected in the fall. No sign of anything. I was at the dinner, which is not always the case for these things. She said the guy in office was just as bad for Topeka as Hoover had been for the country and so would support the candidate. All energetic. We had lunch together, just an hour or so ago. Maria came over with the receipts from the house; they spoke in the parlor, with Maria leaving soon after. Then, all of a sudden, I hear a thud. She's on the floor in the hallway. I knew right away it was over. Her eyes were half open."

"I don't know what I'm going to do, Dad."

"Bobby, we'll get through it. You and me. I'm not going anywhere soon. I'm not that old. Irishmen live long lives."

The funeral was held at the Catholic church across the street from the State Capitol Building where Tom and Barbara had met so many years before. It was packed. Legislators, judges, lawyers, businesspeople, ordinary citizens, men and women, whether they were Catholic or not, as well as dozens of Barbara's friends and all the Tauers of Wamego and Westmoreland, filled the pews. "The lady was loved by many and appreciated by all who knew her," said Bill Adams, former Senator and Vice President to the reporter on the steps of the church after the service. "There was no woman in Topeka, nor maybe anywhere in Kansas, who knew more people and worked more discreetly with whoever asked to get things done for this city and this state," he added. "She was a special lady." Maggie and everyone else in the family from Wamego were stunned at the number of people who were there. "I had no idea," said George. "My chubby little sister who I used to defend back in New York. Combative, stubborn, but so loving, a great mother to Bobby. She always wanted to be someone important. And she did. All these people. I had no idea."

Chapter 32

"Dad, I have to tell you something. You should know." Bob was looking at his father. "Know about what?" asked Tom.

"All about me." The look in his father's eyes told Bob that he realized what he was about to tell him.

"All about you. What are you talking about?"

"Me. Dad. My real mother. My real father. I don't want you hurt by this, but you should know that I know."

"Alright. How did you find out?"

"The papers, Dad. Mom's agreement with Amos Muller. Years ago. The summer I was fourteen. In the attic. Winnie was here. I made her tell me what it was all about and she told me. I had the document in front of me. She made me promise to never tell Mom that I knew. I never did."

"She loved you, Bobby. Like nothing else in her life."

"I loved her too, Dad. She was my Mom. And I was not going to cause her dismay in any way. I'm old enough now to realize just how much Winnie was right, about not telling Mom."

"What do you know, Bobby?

"That Aunt Louise is my real mother. That she died when I was a week old. That Amos signed me over to Mom until he could pay her back. That he never came back. That I was officially adopted when I was seven years old."

"Is that everything?" Tom had to know what his son knew about his real father. Maybe he could avoid the worst.

"What else is there to it?" Bob hesitated. He did not want to tell his father that he knew of the mental illness, the VD.

"That he disappeared. We have no knowledge of where he is. He never came back to get you. He could have. Thank God he didn't. You were his until you were seven. You understand all of that. We were petrified he would come and take you. I think those are things that you should know."

"I know about the adoption. I found those papers as well. I love you, Dad. You will always be Dad. You always have been." He got up, went around the table and put his arms around the slim, dapper little man who had always been his father. "And I'm not going anywhere, Dad. Not back to California. Too far from you. I am going to see K.U. tomorrow. See if I can't transfer for the fall. Bill Townsend told me he thought it could be done. I'll be closer and I'll come home on weekends. My grades are good enough to get in anywhere. In the meantime, I need to go Wamego. Mag is taking this pretty hard."

"Yes, you should. Will told me she has hardly said a word since getting the news. Like in a trance at the funeral. It was not the Mag we know. Went right back to Wamego afterwards."

The call did not last very long. "Don't come, Bob. She doesn't want to see anybody for awhile," said Will.

"Can I speak with her?"

"She won't come to the phone. I can tell you right now."

"Ok. Understand. Give her my love."

200

After getting home from Topeka and the funeral, Mag went around back and found the bench under the big cottonwood. The thoughts came to her. Those times she would come home from school and I would be in the road. Scoop me up in her arms. My big sister. The evenings she would read to me. That doll she made, with the buttons for eyes, the sled for the hill and the snow. Said it was just like when she was a little girl back in Austria. One of her only memories of then. The toys she would send Louise and me from wherever she was. The times she would take us to the circus when it came to Kansas City. The little stuffed elephant. I had that a long time. The arguments over Bobby. I wish we had never had them. Divided us for a long time. So sorry about it. I could have been more accepting. She was a good mother. Bob has turned out so well. Oh, Barbara, I was so mean to you. Forgive me. Forgive me. The phone rang. Will answered. She heard him say she would not come to the phone. "Who was it, Will?"

"It was Bobby."

A few weeks later, Winnie was visiting Topeka on her way to Wamego to see her Mom and Dad. Bob had picked her up at the train station and after getting home, was closing the hood on the car. "Needs oil, I'm afraid. A little low. Need to get to the station. Want to come with me?" he asked Winnie. "Can't take you to Wamego without the oil."

"I told Dad I knew, Winnie, about my birth," as they walked to the station two blocks away. "He seemed relieved. He had tears in his eyes. He hugged me when I told him. Said it was my right to know, but that he was thankful I never told Mom. I refrained from talking about the VD and the mental hospital stuff, but I told him later about that."

"You should probably tell Mag as well that you know about Louise."

"Yeah, I guess so. I was there a month ago. She was still upset about Mom. I think she will be for awhile."

"Yes. The only Tauer sister left. Mag's got her heart on her sleeve."

"I'll tell her I know, but I won't tell her anything about the stuff about Amos."

"Yes, best you don't. You're coming with me tomorrow." said Winnie. "Go see Mag."

"I always do."

Bob dropped Winnie off at George and Mary's, then went to see his aunt. Parking in the driveway, he observed her walking briskly up the hill. "Well, well, Bobby college boy! My dear nephew!" she cried out as she approached. "What brings you here? Came to see me, I hope. That old Ford still seems to work."

"It works fine. Dad's a machinist, so he keeps things running and he doesn't like to spend money he doesn't have to. Just dropped Winnie off. She says hello and will come over later or tomorrow. And yes, I came to see you," he said as he hugged her.

"Lordy be," said Maggie while being embraced. "You come in and have a glass of lemonade. It's hotter than hell. Damned if I have to walk all over town now."

"No more car?"

"No more car. It's been awhile. By the way, aren't you supposed to be on your way back to California, to college? What have you been doing this summer? You only came to see me once. Anyway, come on in and we'll talk inside."

Will was sitting in the living room, reading a newspaper. He looked at Bobby, gave him a nod, then went back to the paper.

"Will's not being nice," said Bobby as he entered into the kitchen with his aunt.

"No. He's not. It's getting worse. Angry. Mean. Gruff. Complains about everything, that nobody around here knows anything. I tell him he's not so smart himself. If he was, he would have a job, some income, and I wouldn't have to scrounge and labor all that I do. Takes away time I would much like to devote to our little plays. Tough times about that. We've been closed for awhile. I'm thinking about resurrecting it, but I don't know. Nobody has any money for leisure, for going out anymore. Anyway, Bobby. I'm glad you're here. We can play some canasta after supper. You will stay over, of course. You can go back tomorrow. Now, what about California? When do you go back?"

"I'm not going back. I'm staying here, close to Dad. I'm at KU starting in September. Transferred everything over."

"You didn't tell me that when you were here for the 4th of July."

"Mag, you weren't really here the 4th of July. You were so affected by Mom's passing. And we didn't stay long, not even for the fireworks. And I wasn't so sure then that I would get into KU. When I decided to do it, it was late for submitting the application for the fall. I just got things confirmed two weeks ago."

"Good. I'm glad, Bobby. You will be closer. I can see you a lot more. You were Barbara's son, but you have been like my own as well."

"Yes. In any case, Mag, I have something to tell you, and it has to do with what you just said, actually. Just as well we talk about it now. Is there a beer somewhere? Lemonade is Ok, but a beer would be so good."

"Of course. I always have a beer stashed away. Let me get it. It's in the cellar. Will doesn't go down there anymore. And you can tell me what this is about, the something you wanted to tell me."

Bob took a swig of beer, then looked at his aunt. "Mag, I know all about my mother. About my real mother. Louise."

"Oh, my Lord." Mag drew her hand to her chest. She looked at Bob, tears forming in her eyes. She took her glasses off and rubbed the lenses with her apron.

"I know and I've known since I was fourteen. I found the agreement between Mom and the man Amos Muller. My real father. I found it in the attic in a box of papers when I was looking for an old toy. Winnie was visiting at the time and told me what happened. She also made me promise to never tell Mom. And I never did."

Mag hesitated, got up, went to the other side of the kitchen, looked out the window for a moment, then turned around, took her glasses off and wiped her eyes. "Oh, my, Bobby. How we all suffered for her. She was such an angel. It is right you know. Yes, she was your mother. She loved you so much." She paused, then looking away from Bob, continued. "She held you just before she died. I have difficulty saying this…It was so sad. She made us promise to look after you. And we have. Your Mom, God Bless Her, took great care of you. We all have."

"Yes, you have."

"You will never know how tragic it was. She died just after you were born. Seven days later."

"Aunt Mag, I know what she died of."

"Difficult childbirth it was."

"No, it was more than that."

"More than that?"

"Venereal disease."

"Oh, my God."

"Three years ago, I found other papers. A doctor's report. I've known since then that Amos Muller gave syphilis to my mother, and that is why she died."

"Oh, my, my, my. I never thought I would have to talk to you about this."

"It is difficult for me to talk about it, but you should know what I am aware of, what I learned. I understood. Mom and Dad were older than the parents of my friends. I wondered about that when I was a boy. I learned why. And I also know that you and Mom fought over who would take me. Winnie told me."

"True. We did fight over you. We got over it, but yes, I wanted you. Louise and I grew up together. Barbara left the farm when we were little. We were so close. I wanted you dearly. Barbara didn't have any children. It was her chance to be a mother and the only one. I gave in."

"You've been a second Mom to me anyway, Mag. You'll be the only one now."

"I guess I will and maybe the longest standing one. I'm glad you have told me this, Bobby. No more secrets amongst us. But thank God you never told your mother."

"I knew I couldn't. I had to tell Dad, though. I couldn't keep it inside anymore, but I only told him a few days after she died. He was glad. No more secrets. Said it was right. And I told him I didn't ever want to see Amos Muller. Ever. But I would like to hear, just this one time, and never bring it up again, Aunt Mag, what was he like?"

"Alright. You should know. As a person, he was not nice. He could be charming. He obviously charmed your mother, who was petrified of ending up an old maid. She so much wanted to have a family. We tried to warn her off. She wouldn't listen. Your dad knew about him. He traveled a lot, working for the railroad. Anyway, he was handsome. Tall, blond like a lot of Germans. He came from Pennsylvania. He said he had no brothers or sisters and said his mother died when he was a boy. That's all I will say, Bobby. There's not much more to tell, in any case. You should not dwell on him. He is somewhere else."

"I know. He's in a mental hospital and has been since a year after my birth."

"My Lord. You do know everything."

"Not so sure about that, but I will say I never ever want to lay eyes on him."

Bob was on the telephone at his fraternity. He had reached the Dauphin County Hospital for the Mentally Ill. It had taken him a week and four calls to telephone companies in Pennsylvania to get the number. He had a bunch of nickels and put them on the ledge next to the pay phone.

"Ma'am, I am a relative of someone who I believe is a patient at your hospital and on behalf of the family, would like to know about his condition, if he is able to read a document, if he is of sound enough mind to do so."

"We don't normally give out information of that nature. Who is the person you believe is here and I will see with the administrator if we can help you."

"His name is Amos Muller."

A moment of hesitation at the other end. "Yes. Mr. Muller," said the woman. "I will have to see. Please wait."

A man came on the line a couple of minutes later. "Hello, I am the deputy administrator of the hospital. You are asking about the condition of one of our patients. Mr. Amos Muller. Is that correct?"

"Yes. I am a relative of his and we need to know if he can sign an important document."

"He is here, but he would not be able to read or sign any document. You could send it here and we would consider it, and decide what to do on his behalf. Patients are often the wards of the hospital with power of attorney. What is the document in question and who am I speaking with?"

Bob had to respond quickly. There was no document. "I am the son of a cousin of his and the document is a release of a mortgage on a property in Illinois that he co-signed with my father years ago."

"Oh, he would not be able to do anything with that."

"What is his condition, then? We have had no news of his condition for a long time. The last time was when he was in a hospital in Kansas."

"He is in deteriorating health. He has little memory, I'm afraid. He is sometimes hysterical."

"Will he ever get out, in your view, Sir? Get back into society?"

"No. He never will. He would not be able to live on his own. He would be a danger to himself as well as to others, I'm afraid." A brief pause, then the man continued. "I have probably told you too much. You say you are the son of a cousin of Mr. Muller's. What is your name?"

Bob had to say something. "Edwards. Richard Edwards. I live in Chicago. I do understand your concern. These matters are sensitive and I appreciate your time. I will be sending you the document. I have the address of the hospital. Thank you."

He'll never get out. I'll never have to deal with him. But he's still my father….. He then dialed another number. "Aunt Mag, Dad and I are coming for Thanksgiving. As always. We should be there Wednesday evening. Got to run." He hung up before Mag could say anything.

Bob and Maggie were at the table. Dinner was over. Tom and Will had gone to the parlor for a cigar. "Mag, Social Security is in place now, you know."

"That's nice, but we don't have access to any of that."

"Well, I may have a way for Will to be eligible for it."

"Fat chance of that. He will need to be working in a job. He hasn't worked in years, ever since he quit working for George. How could he possibly be eligible?"

"Through a job. Maybe we could find him one here in Wamego."

"Bobby, he's 58 years old and they still believe he was involved 20 years ago. Long memories around here. Nobody's going to hire him."

"Would he take a job if I found him one?"

"I doubt it, but you could ask him. And where would you find something for him?"

"I have an idea, but not ready to talk about it yet."

"An idea. Well, when you're ready to talk about it, see him about it."

"Mag, how do you put up with this? You work your butt off and he does nothing."

"I married him. For better or for worse. I could never throw him out, although I've thought of it. Don't you ever repeat that." She looked at Bob, raising her eyebrows, skeptical of anything her nephew would propose for her husband. "Now, what is your idea?"

"Need to check something out. It may not go anywhere."

"OK. You go ahead and check and I will continue to be skeptical. Do you want another piece of pie, my dear nephew?"

The bar had just opened. It was the Saturday morning after Thanksgiving. Bob's summertime buddy from childhood, now the owner, who inherited it from his father, who had died suddenly the year before, was at the end of the bar. Nobody else was in the place as far as Bob could tell. "Bobby, how are you?" said Richie Ebert with a big grin on his face as he came around the end of the bar and gave his old friend a big hug.

"Good to see you, man," replied Bob. "How's business?"

"It's good, actually. Farm prices have improved. Corn's up, so's wheat. Farmers and everybody else have a bit more money. Pool table in the back helps a bit, keeps them in here for an extra beer or two. How's KU?"

"KU's fine. You should be there, by the way. They could use a fullback."

"Could never do it. Dad needed me here. Prohibition was over. We needed to build up the business after the years of it being just a café. Bad knee, anyway. I would not have lasted very long. How's your family? Your aunt? She's a celebrity here, you know. My mom still talks about the radio show."

"Well, she doesn't do much of that anymore. It's been awhile. The theatre has been closed for years."

"I see her from time to time, delivering pies to Jimmy's, for God's sake."

"Actually, it's a reason why I'm here. I need a favor from you, old buddy."

"And, what could that be? I owe you one. That accident. You saved my butt."

Yes, thought Bob. Saved him from big trouble. It was Freddie who stole the car. He said it was Richie. I covered for him, said he was with me. He wasn't, but I knew Richie could never steal a car. Taking the ride with Freddie was his mistake.

"Well, buddies are buddies. You didn't do it and I knew it. Here's what's up. My Uncle Will, Mag's husband. It's about him. I want to find him a job. I thought maybe you could use someone here, even part time. I have no idea. It's a long shot."

"Your uncle. Yes. Wasn't he involved in that bank failure years ago? Kinda what everybody thinks."

"He wasn't involved, but nobody in town believed it. I can tell you he did nothing wrong. He has suffered because of it. Blackballed everywhere. He needs a job. My aunt needs him to find one. Do you need anybody, Richie?"

Richie looked at Bob for a moment before answering. "We've always been buddies. I could. I owe you one. Maybe for filling in on busy nights. I get them, and we sometimes could use some help. Here's what. I'll meet him, at least. I at least owe you that. I'll see. How old is he?"

"He's 58."

"Ooh… 58. Listen. I'll meet him anyway. Have him come in on Monday. I'll see."

"Thank you, buddy. But if it doesn't work, it doesn't work. OK?"

"OK. If it does work out, you owe me a game in Lawrence next fall. Nebraska. Is it a deal?"

"It's a deal." If Will doesn't do this, I'll ream him out, he thought. Even if he is 58.

"Bobby, I'll do it. Ten to fifteen hours a week. I can do that. I'll even be able to see some old friends from time to time. I don't see them much anymore. Maybe make me feel better as well."

"You could use that, that's for sure. You know why I'm doing this, Uncle Will. Trying to help you in these tough times. But it's about you qualifying for social security. What the government brought in a couple years ago. You do this for a few years and you will qualify for some income when you can no longer work at all or when you turn 65."

"Roosevelt stuff."

"Yes. Roosevelt stuff, and thank God he did it."

"You're a good boy, Bobby. I thank you for doing this."

"Well, you should thank Richie. He says he needs someone. The timing was right, he said. Hopefully, it can work and you two will get along."

"I knew his dad. I will do my best. Bartender. Never thought I would do something like that, but.....When would I start?"

"Go see him Monday. It's not a done deal yet. You have to see for yourself, and make the arrangement with Richie." Mag looked at Bobby as she came through the dining room door with dinner. She gave him a big wink.

Chapter 33

Wamego, October, 1938....

Bob parked down the hill. There was nothing available closer. Cars parked all the way up the street. As he walked up the hill, he could see people on the porch, milling about, chatting, shaking hands. *What's this about?* He went up the stairs, found his way in, saw some people he knew, exchanged some good words and greetings, then looked for his aunt.

"Bob, so glad you're here. I want you to meet someone," said a bubbly, almost bouncing Maggie as she worked her way through the crowd and caught her nephew by the elbow.

"Just got here. What's this all about? Celebration about a new play that just made a big hit?"

"No, no, no. It's about the elections coming up. What else? I want you to meet our candidate for Congress. He's here. James Grady. Where is he?" said Mag as she scoured the room. "There he is. Come. And I want to tell you something else when we're done."

Bob immediately recognized the man Mag was leading him to.

"Hello, Sir. Pleased to meet you, but we have met before", said Bob. Grady looked puzzled. "Years ago. In the kitchen of my folks' place in Topeka. Chicken wings… and we talked autographs. You worked for one of the men at the dinner."

"Yes. Bobby. Bobby Hagen. I recognize you now. I was at your mother's that night. The night they cooked up the Vice Presidential thing. Yes. Good to see you."

"And you are the James Grady, candidate for Congress. I heard you work for the President, the current one."

"Yes, I switched. Not long after the '28 election. Long story. Let's just say disillusion set in. Herbert Hoover was not a very good president. He had no idea about how to deal with the Crash. He would not listen to Bill, who would have quit if he had not been such a staunch party guy. And Vice Presidents don't resign. Anyway, I'm here. I believe in Roosevelt and am running for Congress. My old allegiance to Mr. Adams has not seemed to hurt."

"Well, you'll have my vote. I was going to vote Democrat anyway and now that I know that James Grady, the candidate, is the James Grady who introduced me to collecting autographs when I was 10 years old, it just confirms it all."

"Autographs. Well. Excellent. It's fun getting them. I suppose you've got a few. We could compare notes sometime." Before Bob could answer, Grady continued. "Now, your aunt here, the number one advocate for change in all of Wamego, I must say, says you are at KU and are interested in politics. Tells me you have organized a debate group on campus. We should talk sometime."

"Gladly. When are you in Lawrence next?"

"Tuesday, week after next. Rally at the Eldridge Hotel, I think it's at noon. I may have some time just before. We could have a cup of coffee at the hotel."

"How about the fraternity house? Sigma Nu. Not that far from the hotel. You could meet many of the guys there. Need all the votes you can get, right?"

"Right. I can see you have a sense of political opportunity. I'm looking forward to it. Sigma Nu it will be. Hopefully, we can have some private time. I may need some help if I win. Up for that, Bob?"

"Sure. Thank you. But I think you will win."

"We'll see. Now, Mrs. Knecht," finding her off to the right, "who else should I meet here?"

"Richie. Hey, buddy. Glad to see you here." Bob had seen Richie Ebert on the other side of the room, and had motioned to him.

"Yeah, great, Bob... I saw you with Grady. You know him?"

"Well, I guess I do. Years ago, when I was a kid at a dinner at our house in Topeka. Other circumstances. I saw him there, when he was accompanying a guest of my mother's. How's it going with my uncle? Haven't seen you since last year. Is he doin' OK?"

"He's doing fine, Bob. So well that I am making him manager of the bar. Told him that today, before coming over here. You're surprised." Bob was surprised, raising his eyebrows. Richie continued. "Yes. It's worked out, I must say. It will free me up to do more of what I want to do. I'm opening up a farm equipment dealership. It's coming together. Agriculture is on its way back. Now's the time to get set up to take advantage of it. There's this Canadian company, Massey-Harris. Great tractors and other machines. I will be their first dealer in Kansas."

"Will as manager of the bar? My God. That's great. I guess it has worked out." Bob was surprised. He didn't think Will had it in him.

"He's been fine. All that stuff about the bank. Whatever it was, it was a long time ago. We never talked about it. He never brought it up. And nobody else ever brought it up. Some people may have said something, but never to me. And never a cent missing. It would be so easy, and I was worried about it at the start. But no. He has actually found ways to save on costs and he found a snooker table that keeps guys in the bar. Takes longer to play. The guys drink. I don't know what his problem was with other people, but he has been fine with me."

"Richie, you're a good man."

"Hey, I got something else to tell you. Your aunt still makes those pies, right? I see her bringing some to Jimmy from time to time."

"Oh, yes. Her pies. Can't make enough of them, apparently."

"I've got something to talk to you about. Could be interesting."

"What is it?" asked Bob. Richie proceeded to tell Bob what is was about.

"I'll bring it up with her."

Bob then left Richie, said hello and exchanged greetings with other people he had not seen in a long time. He then caught up with Mag, still welcoming others as they came in.

"You know. I saw you with Richie. I'm so glad about Will. So, so glad. Enough income now to get by. But I fear Jimmy will still want pies. And I'll continue to do it. What else am I going to do with my days? Anyway, I'm happy. All because of you, Bobby." Bob looked at her and decided he would speak to her about Richie's proposal later on. "See some people I know. Good get-together, Mag." Mag looked at Bob as he was being pulled away to acknowledge someone else he had known during those summers in Wamego. I'm going to talk to Grady. Bobby must get into politics. A natural. A worthy Tauer. Grady could find something for him to do. Get his feet wet. Bobby Hagen, President of the United States! Why not? I'll write a play about it. The kid who had three mothers who became President!

A half hour later, after Grady had spoken and had thanked everyone for being there and had thanked Margaret Knecht for the hospitality and the opportunity to meet the people of Wamego, Frances found Bobby. "You've done good, Bob. Dad has his self-respect back. Ebert's an OK guy. God bless you. God bless it all."

"I'm just glad it's working out. And how are you?"

"I'm fine."

"You heard from Winnie? Been a while for me. She used to be here two, three times during the year."

"Well, she's married now. Been a year with Jack. He does screen writing. The movies. She helps him and I understand they're buying a flower shop. She's happy."

Bob looked at Frances as she was talking. 32 now. Living at home. Paying the bills all these years. Working for that damn optometrist who takes advantage of her. Needs to stop. She could tell some guy she could marry him. She's an attractive woman. The depression. Such a toll. Mag, Will, Frances. Everybody. This whole town.

Frances looked around, said good-bye to a neighbor as they walked toward the door, then came back to where Bobby was.

"You know, Mom keeps making those pies. She's always afraid Will will do something to lose the job so she doesn't dare quit. In the meantime, she's getting requests from grocery stores in Alma, and the one in Belvue down the road."

"Oh, yeah? Alma and Belvue. Interesting."

The next day after dinner, Will went to the parlor to have a cigar. Bob grabbed Mag's wrist before she could get up from the table. "Got something to talk to you about. Sit back down." Maggie looked at Bob with a quizzical expression. "Frances tells me you're getting requests for pies from Alma. The grocery store there, and apparently from Belvue as well. Seems like you're getting some extra demand. I'm not surprised. They're pretty good, like no others. You could gear up to supply those folks, Mag."

"Oh, come on. How could I do that? I have enough trouble supplying the grocery store here."

"Well, Richie Ebert told me something else yesterday. He said he had discovered that one of those abandoned stores at the end of Main Street by the tracks, you know which ones I mean on the east side, had a big oven in the back. His Dad had bought the place years ago for almost nothing, but had not found anything to do with it. The Depression. Said he thought somebody made bread there years ago, judging by the looks of it when you go into the back of it. From the front, it looks like just about any old retail shop that's been closed for years. I'm sure you know it. Well, there's a big oven in the back. Anyway, he said he thought the oven could still work and there were some tables and counters back there that could be put into shape. Said he thought you could make pies there. Just an idea, he said. So I said, let's go see it. He took me over there today and we went in. Lots of stuff strewn about, but sure enough, there was a big wood-fired oven, and a decent work place. I asked him what he would want if we wanted to rent it. Said not much, as long as whoever rented it paid for the fix-up. Said it was not generating any revenue now, so anything would be better."

"And you think I could rent that place and do the pies from there? Are you crazy, Bobby? That will take money that I don't have."

At that moment, Frances came in the back door, arriving after work, and saw that Maggie and Bob were in a big-time discussion.

Bob turned around and said before Frances could say anything "Frances. I've got a proposition for you and your mother. A business proposition. Sit down. Let me explain."

"Why are you bringing Frances into this? She has nothing to do with the pie stuff."

"Well, maybe she should. Frances, those requests from Alma and elsewhere you told me about. I have a solution for it. A solution that may be of interest to you, as well. Get you out of that damn job with the optometrist."

"Business proposition. Pies for Alma. Me involved. What the hell are you talking about?" asked Frances.

Four months later, Maggie's Pies opened on Main Street. George Tauer had gone to work on the premises. There was a new front door and new plate window frames, a sanded and polished wood floor, with new lighting and freshly plastered walls. People were saying they had never seen that block look so rejuvenated with the new look on the corner. The oven proved to be workable. Orders were coming in from Alma, from Rossville and as far away as Westmoreland. Will had found an abandoned 1931 Ford delivery van in a backyard in Wabaunsee and had one of the patrons of the bar fix it up. A paint job was done with one of Andreas Tauer's sons painting Maggie's Pies – Wamego with great renditions of steaming pies on the side panels. Frances had quit her job and had taken over as business manager of the enterprise. Enough orders had started to come in for Mag to hire a woman from the parish women's group to help her with baking. Another of Andreas' sons drove the delivery truck. Within six months of opening, Maggie's Pies was supplying freshly-baked apple and cherry pies to grocery stores in eight other towns.

By the summer of 1941, Maggie no longer had to beat and roll the dough and sweat before the oven. She had other people to do that. At 61, she could finally start to relax. Frances ran the business. As to Will, he had not quit the job at Richie's tavern as everybody thought he eventually would. He had his self-esteem back and was less the grumpy old man of before. He stayed on the job and became once again a center of information on what was happening in town. Lawyers and judges were coming to the tavern for lunch, something that never happened before, and bringing other people with them. Things were looking good. Prosperity was coming back to Wamego. Maggie could turn her attention to other things, and she did. By the fall of 1941, she had written updates of the most popular episodes of 'Mom and Pop of Adams Creek Road' the comedy series that played in Wamego and on the radio a decade earlier.

Then the war came to America on December 7. Pearl Harbor.

Chapter 34

December 1945....

The train was a half-hour out of Kansas City, on its way to Chicago. The young Army officer was sitting across from a man in a Navy lieutenant's uniform. "Where you headed, Navy man, if you don't mind me asking?" said the army captain.

"Don't mind at all. Going to Quebec City, by way of Chicago and other points, to get my bride," replied Bob Hagen. "War's over. Time to get on with life. What about you?"

"Home to Milwaukee. Taking the uniform off in Chicago. Yep. Getting on with life. Marrying a Canadian, huh?"

"Already married. Did it on leave in '43 before shipping out to the Pacific. She stayed with her folks in the meantime."

"How did you meet up with a Canadian girl? You're from Kansas City, I gather. It's a long way away," said the Army man.

"From Topeka. But you're right. A long way away. It all started with a trip to Canada with my folks when I was a kid. I loved the warmth of the people and the exoticness of the language and beauty of the city so different from where we lived. Told myself I would go back some day. Well, I was in the insurance business in Kansas in '41 before we got into the war and went to a convention in Quebec City that summer, and sure enough, met a girl. Wonderful girl. Blind date for a dance at the big hotel there. Spent as much time as I could the next three days with her before the convention was over. Wanted to marry her then, but her dad said no. Couldn't blame him. But I was hooked. The war came with Pearl and I enlisted, but I never forgot her. We wrote. The war was on. I got to officer's training, then was stationed in a variety of places. The correspondence dropped off, then one day I heard from the wife of one of my insurance pals that the girl was engaged to some guy in Quebec. Oh boy, I couldn't let that happen, so I called her on the telephone and said I was coming to marry her. I had a leave scheduled for a month later. She said yes. So, I went to Quebec and we did it. Big French-Canadian wedding. Never saw so many people who could be in the same family. So, here I am, on my way to get her and bring her back to Kansas."

"French-Canadian? You going to have to speak French?"

"Maybe, if she tells me I have to."

"Must be something."

"Yes, she is." The conductor came by, asked them for their tickets. There were many other servicemen on the train. All going home. The war was over.

As the conductor moved on, the army captain looked at Bob's uniform and observed the service bars. "Where did you serve?"

"Pacific. Landed troops on islands. I ended up with a squadron of LCTs, then in Japan for two months. Part of the occupation. Bad news that was. What about you? I see you're Airborne."

"41st Airborne. In Italy, then in France. Lost a lot of buddies. Our drops didn't always get us into the places we were

222

supposed to go to, but I made it through. I was in occupation as well. Munich and the area bordering Czechoslovakia, watching the Russians. By the way, my name is Tom. Tom Schultz."

"Bob Hagen. Pleased to meet you, Tom. You outrank me. I should be calling you sir."

"No. This is over. We just happen to be still wearing our uniforms. So, you were in insurance before the war? How was that?"

"It was fine. Got me a wife, for one. Going back to it. Got started in it my last year in college. Saw so much hardship in the 30's when people close to the family died and their kids and families were destitute. A former Congressman introduced me to the head agent in Kansas for one of the companies. I was still in college, so when I met him he asked me to write him an essay on the importance of insurance. I wrote up the stories of the families who had had none. Made the case how they could have afforded it. I didn't really know what I was talking about, but he said I was hired and so I started the day after graduation in '39."

"Kansas. Kansas University?" asked the army captain.

"Yes. A Jayhawk. How about you?"

"Marquette. Jesuit school in Milwaukee."

"I know that, and I think you played basketball, did you not? I remember a Tom Schultz playing against Kansas once at a game in Kansas City."

"That's me. You have a good memory. We lost that one. Kansas was always good."

"Well, usually. The inventor of basketball, and a Canadian, by the way, was the coach at Kansas for awhile. The team has had a lot to live up to... But I'll be. You're the same guy. I remember that Schultz being a short guy who had a deadly shot."

"I'm still short." He stood up, brushed off his uniform. "This is Tom Schultz, Marquette guard, '37 to '39, and five foot six."

The two spent the next few hours talking and exchanging stories, all the way to Chicago. Addresses and home phone numbers were exchanged as the train pulled into the station. They talked about their interests in politics. Tom Schultz proved to be just as into it as Bob was. The two would develop a friendship and would remain lifelong friends...and more.

Bob got to Quebec two days later. Snow was on the ground, lots of it, with the wind howling outside the palatial old train station that resembled a small castle. His bride, Estelle, accompanied by her father, Elphège, an elegant gentleman who was also an insurance man, met Bob as he emerged into the domed central hall of the station. With his white officer's cap and immaculate dark blue uniform with the bars and the officer's stripes, Bob cut an impressive figure. People turned and watched the embrace of the lovely girl and her dashing officer husband.

Four days later, they were at a family party with over a hundred people in attendance in a reception hall next to the church in the small village across the river from Quebec City where they had been married two years before. It had been announced to family and Estelle's friends as a belated wedding celebration and the return of Bob to collect his bride. Bob was asked at the reception by someone in his wife's extended family, how it all happened. "Decided on getting a wife here when I was twelve years old. I'm serious," responded Bob.

"Twelve years old? You met Estelle when she was a little girl?" asked the man.

"No, but I decided then that here was where I would find my wife, and when I had the chance, when I came back years ago, I met Estelle, was smacked by her, and I went through with my promise to myself."

"The American way. You are very American."

"I guess I am. Happy we're doing this here. I don't have a family big like this back home," said Bob, extending his arms out towards the crowd in the reception hall.

"Well, you have one here now. There are a few of us. Just don't take Estelle away from here forever."

"I won't."

Back in Kansas, Maggie was itching to meet Bobby's lady. She would have to wait. His Christmas would be in Quebec. She was overjoyed and relieved that Bob had survived the war. She held him closely when he came home. Tom, his Dad, had died when Bob was overseas. He had no one else to come home to, at least in Kansas. The family in Wamego was it. When he enlisted, as she knew he would, she was scared he wouldn't make it. The boys were getting killed and losing battles in the Pacific. The Japanese were overrunning everything. The disaster of Pearl Harbor had hit home. One of Bob's high school buddies was on the Oklahoma, and never made it out. Father Bieler, her parish priest, lost a nephew who had spent his summers in Wamego. The boy had buddied with Bob, playing baseball together for the local Pony League team and introduced Bob to tennis, before he would be good enough to be tennis instructor at a Topeka country club during his college summers.

Her thoughts turned to the other women in the family. Winnie. Living happily in California. With Jack, her funny, jokester husband who knows all those people in the movie business and loves her. What a couple they make. The flower shop in Pasadena. Her brothers close by and now George living out there. Eighty-eight. Still going strong. First Christmas of my life that George is not around. Just him and me now from the Tauers. To her daughter. Frances. She's found her man, thank God. Roscoe. What a fine guy. And with that big farm. She can run the business without any financial worries. Roscoe wants her to continue. Business is going well.

"Well, what are you going to do now?" asked Maggie

"What do you mean?" Bob and Mag were in her kitchen after Sunday dinner, doing the dishes and preparing for a game of canasta while Frances and Estelle were out for a walk. Will and Roscoe were in the parlor for a post-dinner cigar.

"About politics? What else?" said Maggie.

"Aunt Mag, I just got back. I'm getting used to being married, getting to know my wife, getting over the war, I have to get back to earning a living and you're asking me about politics?"

"Yes, I am. Now is the time to get back into it. You helped Grady before the war. Now it's time for him to help you. I spoke to him about it."

"You did what? Spoke to Grady about helping me? For what?"

"For you running for State Senator. The Topeka Senate seat is open. The election is in November. You have plenty of time to organize."

"Organize? I don't have any money for that and I don't have the experience, either. I need to get back into insurance and earn a living. I can't do this."

"Yes, you can. The company is taking you back, they have already promoted you, and Grady says he'll find you the money for a campaign."

"Mag, you're going way too far on this. Estelle won't appreciate it. We're trying to start a family."

"I already spoke to her about it. She has politics in her family. Her uncle was a government minister or other up there. She said it was one of the best things that happened to her family, brought them out of a backwater mentality, she called it."

"You spoke to her? About politics?"

"No. I didn't speak to her. I wrote to her and she wrote back. Over a year ago, when you were in the Pacific. I wrote her about you, how proud we all were and how glad we were to have her in the family, that I was sure you would make it through the war, that you were coming back to her. In reality, I worried about that, but that's what I told her anyway. I wrote about what you were about, and where you could go in life. She wrote and said she was glad I shared that with her. Then she mentioned her uncle and the family's involvement in politics. And about wanting a big family. Said she was used to it all. Excellent English, by the way."

"She grew up in an English-French town in New Brunswick. Taught English before I met her. But you two were exchanging letters? She never told me about that."

"Collusion of the females, Bobby. Goes back a ways with the Tauers. Get used to it."

Bob Hagen ran for State Senator the following November, won the Democratic nomination, but lost in a close race to the Republican, who was twice his age and had been the Topeka district attorney for years. It would not be over, but at 29 he had a wife to love, a family to build and a business to grow.

Epilogue

Fourteen years later…..November 1960…

Maggie was on the porch with a shawl around her shoulders and a blanket over her legs. It was almost not necessary. The evening was warm for November. The sunset sky to the west was red, orange, yellow, a stunning view of color, rising up above the slopes of autumn colored grass. It was four days after the election. Bobby had won. Bob Hagen, Governor of the State of Kansas. I knew he would do it, she thought. I always knew he could. Louise would be so proud. So would Barbara and Poppa, who never knew his grandson. The celebrations. Almost too much, but I would not have missed them for the world. Hagen House. Just as much Tauer House. Now the governor's place. Right across the street from the Statehouse. As if Barbara knew it would come to this. He is blessed. A wonderful wife. Four beautiful kids. The cancer. It went away, somehow. Treatment. Seven years now. Hodgkin's. Doctor said it probably came from the war and could come back. Probably had more to do with what was transmitted to Louise. We'll probably never know. Whatever happened to that vile man? Bobby won't talk about it.

He did it. All those people who said it couldn't be done. All the help he had. The Catholics. What would we have done without the Catholics of Kansas? Kennedy winning. Bobby part of it. So be it. He will be a good governor. Too bad Will isn't around. He would be proud of the boy, despite his old grumpy self. Saved him from

229

his own oblivion with the job he found for him. He would have spoken endlessly to the boys down at the depot. My man, faults and all.

She thought of where she spent her childhood. Country Farm Road. Five miles that way, just over those hills. Where I met Will. My Indian friends. All gone now. Must go to the cemetery. The spirits. They will always be there.

She looked off to the right, up the lane toward the stable and saw Frances with Roscoe walking back to the house.

She found a good man, after all. This farm, really more a ranch now. Three thousand acres. All you can see in every direction, he says whenever anybody asks.

She runs the business now, basically always has. Maggie's Pies. Same recipe. Apple and Cherry. I don't have to go there anymore. 'Wamego's Famous Maggie's Pies'. Same old crust recipe, never to be divulged. Topeka, Manhattan, Salina, Junction City. You can buy them all over.

The theatre, the radio show, they were dumn, funny stories, but they worked. 25 cents admission. Could you believe it? Our comedy hours from the dustbowl. It's coming back now. Helen's granddaughter discovering a couple of scripts in her attic and deciding to get it going again. Said she would invite Bobby to open it up in January. A new Wamego Comedy Playhouse.

Frances saw Mag on the porch and came and sat next to her.

"Deep in thought, Mom?"

"Yes. It was quite a week."

"And quite a life. I can tell when you go there." Frances paused a moment, looking out at the sunset, then turned towards

230

her mother. "Hey....something I wanted to ask you. At the big house the other night, the party afterwards with all those people, I noticed you speaking with someone and looking at the two paintings on the wall. Those old paintings Barbara kept up there. You were pointing at them. What was that all about?"

"The man, who I don't know, never met, asked me if I knew who the man was in those paintings. I told him it was somebody who helped all this happen. A long time ago."

The Sisters

Maggie   Barbara   Louise

Tom Creary